GLOBALVIEWPOINTS

Aging

Other Books of Related Interest:

At Issue Series
Extending the Human Lifespan
Right to Die

Global Viewpoints Series
Mental Illness

Opposing Viewpoints Series
The Aging Population
Alternative Medicine

GLOBALVIEWPOINTS

Aging

Noah Berlatsky, Book Editor

GREENHAVEN PRESS
A part of Gale, Cengage Learning

GALE
CENGAGE Learning·

Farmington Hills, Mich • San Francisco • New York • Waterville, Maine
Meriden, Conn • Mason, Ohio • Chicago

Elizabeth Des Chenes, *Director, Content Strategy*
Cynthia Sanner, *Publisher*
Douglas Dentino, *Manager, New Product*

© 2014 Greenhaven Press, a part of Gale, Cengage Learning

WCN: 01-100-101

Articles in Greenhaven Press anthologies are often edited for length to meet page requirements. In addition, original titles of these works are changed to clearly present the main thesis and to explicitly indicate the author's opinion. Every effort is made to ensure that Greenhaven Press accurately reflects the original intent of the authors. Every effort has been made to trace the owners of copyrighted material.

Cover image © Alan Bailey/Shutterstock.com.

LIBRARY OF CONGRESS CATALOGING-IN-PUBLICATION DATA

Aging / Noah Berlatsky, book editor.
    pages cm. -- (Global viewpoints)
    Includes bibliographical references and index.
    ISBN 978-0-7377-6902-9 (hardcover) -- ISBN 978-0-7377-6903-6 (pbk.)
    1. Older people--Cross-cultural studies. 2. Aging--Cross-cultural studies. I. Berlatsky, Noah.
    HQ1061.A42454 20104
    305.26--dc23
                                                                    2013036321

Printed in Mexico
1 2 3 4 5 6 7 18 17 16 15 14

Contents

China's one-child policy and changing living patterns
mean the elderly often have no support structure. This is
becoming a serious social problem as the population
ages.

Chapter 2: Policy Solutions to Aging Populations

Chapter 3: Attitudes toward the Elderly

Chapter 4: Health Issues and Aging

High death rates from AIDS among the young in Africa have left many elderly people without any relatives to care for them.

Foreword

> "The problems of all of humanity can
> only be solved by all of humanity."
> —Swiss author Friedrich Dürrenmatt

Global interdependence has become an undeniable reality. Mass media and technology have increased worldwide access to information and created a society of global citizens. Understanding and navigating this global community is a challenge, requiring a high degree of information literacy and a new level of learning sophistication.

Building on the success of its flagship series, Opposing Viewpoints, Greenhaven Press has created the Global Viewpoints series to examine a broad range of current, often controversial topics of worldwide importance from a variety of international perspectives. Providing students and other readers with the information they need to explore global connections and think critically about worldwide implications, each Global Viewpoints volume offers a panoramic view of a topic of widespread significance.

Drugs, famine, immigration—a broad, international treatment is essential to do justice to social, environmental, health, and political issues such as these. Junior high, high school, and early college students, as well as general readers, can all use Global Viewpoints anthologies to discern the complexities relating to each issue. Readers will be able to examine unique national perspectives while, at the same time, appreciating the interconnectedness that global priorities bring to all nations and cultures.

Material in each volume is selected from a diverse range of sources, including journals, magazines, newspapers, nonfiction books, speeches, government documents, pamphlets, organization newsletters, and position papers. Global Viewpoints is truly global, with material drawn primarily from international sources available in English and secondarily from US sources with extensive international coverage.

Features of each volume in the Global Viewpoints series include:

- An **annotated table of contents** that provides a brief summary of each essay in the volume, including the name of the country or area covered in the essay.

- An **introduction** specific to the volume topic.

- A **world map** to help readers locate the countries or areas covered in the essays.

- For each viewpoint, an **introduction** that contains notes about the author and source of the viewpoint explains why material from the specific country is being presented, summarizes the main points of the viewpoint, and offers three **guided reading questions** to aid in understanding and comprehension.

- **For further discussion** questions that promote critical thinking by asking the reader to compare and contrast aspects of the viewpoints or draw conclusions about perspectives and arguments.

- A worldwide list of **organizations to contact** for readers seeking additional information.

- A **periodical bibliography** for each chapter and a **bibliography of books** on the volume topic to aid in further research.

- A comprehensive **subject index** to offer access to people, places, events, and subjects cited in the text, with the countries covered in the viewpoints highlighted.

Global Viewpoints is designed for a broad spectrum of readers who want to learn more about current events, history, political science, government, international relations, economics, environmental science, world cultures, and sociology—students doing research for class assignments or debates, teachers and faculty seeking to supplement course materials, and others wanting to understand current issues better. By presenting how people in various countries perceive the root causes, current consequences, and proposed solutions to worldwide challenges, Global Viewpoints volumes offer readers opportunities to enhance their global awareness and their knowledge of cultures worldwide.

Introduction

"Thailand is experiencing unparalleled growth of its older population, in number and proportion. This growth has been faster than most developed countries and the second fastest in South-East Asia, next to Singapore. This turnabout in the population dynamic has shifted a spotlight onto the issue of ageing and has revealed a need for substantial research and policy attention."

—*Rika Fujioka and Sopon Thangphet, "Decent Work for Older Persons in Thailand," February 2009*

Thailand has one of the most quickly aging populations in Southeast Asia, second only to Singapore. The percentage of people over sixty in the country more than doubled from 1975, when it stood at 5 percent, to 2012, when it reached 12 percent. Projections by the United Nations suggest that the number of Thais over sixty will continue to increase and may reach more than 50 percent by 2050.

As in other parts of Asia, the rapid increase in the elderly population has been spurred by a number of factors. One of these is falling birthrates. In the 1970s, Thai families had an average of five or six children; today they have, on average, just one. Improvements in health care have also led to longer life spans. In 1941 Thai life expectancy was fifty-two years old; today it is seventy-four, a jump of more than twenty years. The combination of fewer children and more elderly is profoundly changing Thailand's demographics and will have an enormous impact on its future.

Its aging workforce confronts Thailand with a number of problems and challenges. One of the most important of these is poverty among the elderly. Those over sixty in Thailand are working more than in the past; most of them work in excess of fifty hours a week, which is the same as younger workers. But a 2009 study by the International Labour Organization (ILO) found that the elderly receive much lower wages than the young. As a result, older people are particularly susceptible to poverty. In fact, the study found that 14 percent of the elderly live in poverty, as compared to 9.6 percent of the population as a whole. The government, in an effort to ameliorate the situation, does have a universal pension scheme. However, this amounts to only 500 Baht, or about $16 a month, far short of what the elderly need to live.

Poverty for the elderly is a particular problem in rural areas. A May 8, 2011, article at Voice of America looked at the northern community of Khon Kaen and found that older people there often are left behind to struggle as younger Thais travel to jobs in city factories. Meanwhile, farms are becoming more and more mechanized, requiring less manpower and leaving fewer jobs for the old. Yet, many of the aging "want to work, because they don't want to be a burden also, and they want to remain to be valued by their community or family," according to Sopon Thangphet of Chiang Mai University.

Such problems led Rika Fujioka, one of the authors of the ILO study, to express concern about Thailand's future. She noted that the number of people over sixty-five in Thailand would double in twenty years—an unprecedented increase. "The implications of such a rapid change are not yet fully understood," she noted. "What's more, their vulnerability means that older persons are likely to be among those most severely affected by the current financial crisis [of 2008–2009]. These are issues that policy makers must address."

How policy makers should address them, however, is an open question. The ILO study suggested that the Thai government try to expand sectors where the elderly could work and to promote employment opportunities for older workers. The ILO also suggested that more money might need to be spent on social security schemes, including community-based programs. In fact, Thailand has already taken steps in this direction. In 1997 Thailand gave older persons in poverty the right to receive state aid. In addition, Abhisit Vejjajiva, Thai prime minister from 2008–2011, pledged to support and encourage local welfare systems.

Another policy possibility suggested by some analysts is to delay the official retirement age. This was set at sixty in 1941 and had not been changed for decades. The low retirement age has become not only a financial problem, but also a logistical one. The average age of civil servants in the Thai government, for example, has crept up and up, and there is concern that as workers retire, there will not be enough new workers coming in to maintain services. To address these issues, a 2008 Civil Service Act extended the retirement age for civil servants, doctors, lawyers, and others with vital technical skills. The extension pushed retirement to sixty-four, with workers able to take two three-year renewals to a maximum of seventy.

Thailand is considering further alterations to civil service retirement. They may extend the seventy-year limit to more workers, or they might simply raise the retirement age to sixty-two across the board for all civil servants. Either way, the secretary-general of the Office of the Civil Service Commission, Nontikorn Kanjanajitra, was quoted as saying that some change is unavoidable, in a December 3, 2012, article in the *National*. "The age gap will only widen, as many civil servants age while we freeze the workforce periodically," he said. "We need to seriously rethink the recruitment rules. There must be incentives to facilitate the return of the recently retired to the public service."

The demographic difficulties that Thailand faces are shared by many countries in the region—such as Japan and Korea.

They are also familiar problems in Europe and, for that matter, throughout the world. The remainder of this book examines issues of aging and the elderly in chapters focusing on the effect of aging populations on society; policy solutions to aging populations; attitudes toward the elderly; and health issues pertaining to aging. As in Thailand, so in all parts of the world—scholars, commenters, and policy makers are trying to determine how best to respond to, care for, and live with a graying population.

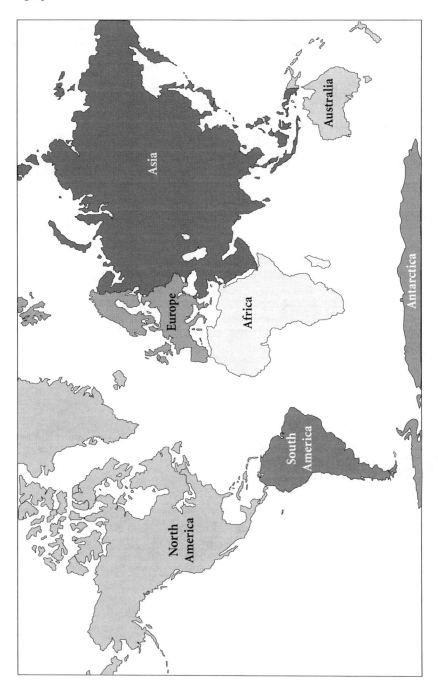

The Effect of Aging Populations on Society

The Effects of an Aging Society in the United Kingdom Are Uncertain

Adam P. Smith

Adam P. Smith is a writer and researcher who has worked with the Optimum Population Trust, which is presently known as Population Matters. In the following viewpoint, Smith notes that Britain's population is aging due to a combination of lower fertility rates and lengthened life expectancy. He says that this will have important effects on many areas of society, including pensions, health care, education, and the economy. However, Smith concludes, the exact effects of an aging population are difficult to predict because of the many uncertain variables.

As you read, consider the following questions:

1. What statistics does Smith provide about fertility rates from 1964 to 2008?

2. What steps has the United Kingdom taken to deal with the problems of pensions and the aging population?

3. What two things does Smith say make it difficult to estimate how much long-term care will be needed in the future?

Adam P. Smith, "Is It Feasible for the UK to Move Towards a Sustainable Population by 2050 While Supporting an Ageing Society?," Optimum Population Trust, August 2010, pp. 5–8.

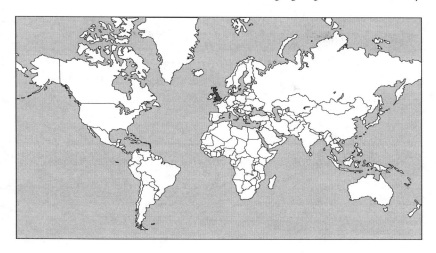

Just as individuals age, it is possible for entire populations to age. This can happen as the average age increases or a larger share of the population is elderly. If a society were to have stable fertility rates and mortality rates, then the population would increase or decrease at a constant rate, but the *age structure would remain constant.* Yet the UK [United Kingdom] today has an ageing population. After the Second World War people started having larger families—the total fertility rate was almost 3 in 1964. This created a large generation known as the baby boomers. At the same time, because of advances in medicine and public health, mortality rates were dropping and therefore life expectancy was improving.

Longer Lives, Fewer Births

The total fertility rate began to decline in the 1970s and has hovered near 1.8 from 1975 until the mid-2000s. Since then it has risen to 1.96 in 2008. During this time, life expectancy has been continuously improving. The combination of relatively fewer births and people living longer is what has led to the ageing population in the UK today.

Dependency ratios [the number of dependents, young and old, divided by the working age population] tell a similar story. From the mid-1970s through 2006 the old-age dependency ratio (defining those aged 16 to pension age as the workforce) stayed near 30 percent. It is currently around 31.5 percent, and ignoring the planned increase in the pension age, . . . by 2050 the old-age dependency ratio would jump to almost 50 percent.

A combination of the baby boom, increasing life expectancy, and decreasing fertility have led to an ageing population in the UK.

Finally, immigration has played a large role in the growth of the UK's population for the past 15 years. At least as far back as 1975 until 1998 there was never a year where net migration was greater in magnitude than 100,000. In fact the overall impact on the UK's population from migration between 1975 and 1994 was essentially zero. Beginning around 1998 immigration increased greatly and net migration averaged almost 180,000 persons per year between 1998 and 2008. 1998 was also the first year where immigration played a larger role in the growing population than the natural increase. Immigration plays an important role in determining the size and structure of a population, but it is highly uncertain. Net migration could be larger in the future, or it could go back towards zero or even negative. This analysis will attempt to take account of this uncertainty.

To summarise, a combination of the baby boom, increasing life expectancy, and decreasing fertility have led to an ageing population in the UK. In the near future baby boomers will be retiring in large numbers, and it may have a big impact on society. . . .

Effect on Society of an Ageing Population

There are many effects that an ageing population has on society. Obvious examples are increased costs of pensions and health care. Less obvious are items such as increased volunteering (retired people have more time to give) or changes in who provides child care (pensioners may be willing to look after their grandchildren). This report focuses more on issues where the connection with ageing is better understood and more data is available not necessarily because they are more important, but because it makes comparing different population profiles easier and more effective. . . .

Pensions

Pensions are one area that will obviously be affected by an increase in the elderly population. Happily, the UK government has been very proactive about the issue. The female state pension age is set to rise to 65, from 60, by adding one year every two years until 2020. By then, both males and females will be eligible for the state pension at 65. Between 2024 and 2046 the pension age is set to slowly rise to 68 years for both men and women. Furthermore, as of this writing [in 2010], the current government is considering raising the retirement age sooner. Simply as a matter of public finances, these increases in the retirement age will make pension funding more sustainable. The old-age dependency ratio for 2050 mentioned in the last section was based on no increase in the pension age. When that increase is factored in, the expected old-age dependency ratio for 2050 becomes a more reasonable 34 percent.

Health care in the last year of life is very expensive.

However, the goal of pension reform is not just to ensure fiscal sustainability for the government, but also to encourage workers to stay in the labour force longer. Simply increasing the state pension age may not achieve this goal. Part of the decision of when to retire is "when the desired level of wealth is accumulated". Naturally the ability to draw a state pension has an increase in a person's wealth, but the fixed age of retirement may be a problem. Some economists think that instead of governments trying to delay retirement, they should encourage each person to retire at an age in line with social costs and benefits. One way to achieve that is to have pensions that allow early retirement with lower benefits or later retirement with higher benefits depending on how much the worker has paid into the pension system. As the pension age increases are happening, right now it is difficult to say how they will affect the retirement decision of older workers. . . .

Health Care

An ageing population will certainly have an effect on the health care system. There are many important interconnections between ageing and health care, and only the most pertinent will be discussed here. The effects of an ageing population on health care change greatly depending on whether there is an expansion or compression of morbidity [that is, sickness or illness]. Expansion of morbidity means that as life expectancy increases, healthy life expectancy increases by a smaller amount, and therefore people are sicker for longer. For example, life expectancy has increased by four years, but healthy life expectancy has only increased by two years. Compression of morbidity is the opposite; healthy life expectancy increases more than the increase in overall life expectancy and people are sick for less time. The effects on health costs can be large: In forecasts that assume the expansion of morbidity, future health costs increase greatly, whereas costs tend to be more manageable if the compression of morbidity is assumed. [M.] Caley and [K.] Sidhu examined increases in overall life expectancy and healthy life expectancy in the UK for the past 25 years; they found that healthy life expectancy had increased at about 72% of the rate of overall life expectancy (2010). This suggests an expansion of morbidity, but not by the full amount of the increase in life expectancy. Of course this does not say what will happen in the future, but only what has happened in the past.

Another problem with health care related to population ageing is that health care in the last year of life is very expensive. This causes problems for cost projections that assume that age-specific health costs will stay constant into the future. For example, the costs for 70- to 75-year-olds today include a lot of the costs of the last year of life. Yet in the future not as many 70- to 75-year-olds will be dying, assuming life expectancy continues to increase. One way to counteract this effect is to increase the cost age-bands by the expected increase in healthy life expectancy, which is the method proposed by Caley and Sidhu (2010). As an example, assume healthy life expectancy is estimated to increase at one year per decade: then in ten years 81- to 86-year-olds would have the same health costs as 80- to 85-year-olds do today.

Also of interest is looking at drivers of increasing health costs in the past. Many researchers have noted that historically technology and increased use of care have played a larger role in increasing costs than demographics. It should be noted, however, that these studies were examining a period with a much smaller increase in the number of elderly people than is predicted to occur in the next 40 years.

Long-Term Care and Disability

Long-term care is another area that will be greatly affected by the increase in the number of elderly people. It is administered to those, primarily the old, who need help not only with medical care, but also with social and personal needs, such as getting dressed. There are several difficulties in measuring how much will be needed in the future. First, unlike most medical care, many of the tasks necessary to help the elderly can and are performed by people with no specialised training. These informal carers, as they are known, play an important role in reducing the demand for government-provided long-term care and will have an important role in containing long-term care costs in the future.

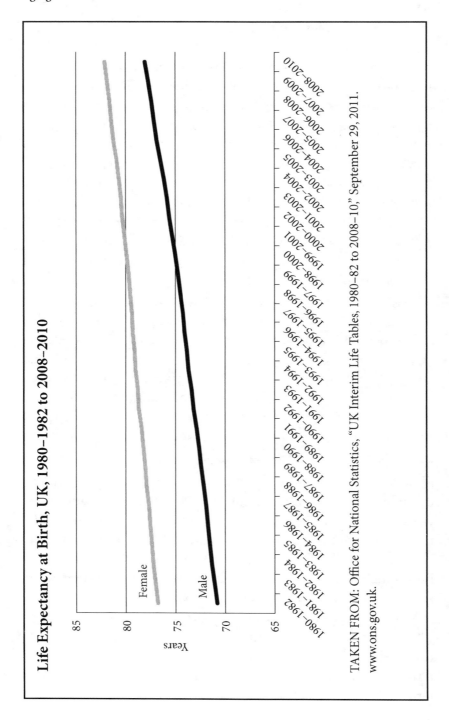

Life Expectancy at Birth, UK, 1980–1982 to 2008–2010

TAKEN FROM: Office for National Statistics, "UK Interim Life Tables, 1980–82 to 2008–10," September 29, 2011. www.ons.gov.uk.

The second thing that makes long-term care difficult to forecast is estimating who will need it. Almost everyone needs a doctor in her life, but a large number of people never need long-term care. One of the problems is that disability is hard to define clearly. Current government statistics primarily rely on asking people if they consider themselves disabled. This can be useful for some measures, but it is not helpful at predicting how much assistance they will need. The last systematic effort to determine how prevalent disability is in the UK took place in the 1980s, and much has changed since then.

If health costs go up because of ageing, but education costs go down because of fewer students, then the net impact on the government would be less than the increase in health costs alone would suggest.

The twin problems of not knowing how much care will be provided informally or knowing how many people may need care in the first place makes projecting future long-term care costs highly uncertain. However, the government has tried: The total spent on long-term care is set to grow from around one percent of GDP [gross domestic product] today to about two percent in 2050. Even though it is still low as a percent of GDP, this doubling of cost could play an important role in future government spending. If costs or demand increase more than expected, then it could cause many problems.

Education

Education may seem like a strange item to include when considering the effects of an ageing population, but it is important for two reasons. The first is that the total cost of education should be lower if there are fewer students. The second is how the education system may be different with fewer students and how that affects society. In terms of cost, any decrease in the cost of education must be considered against increases in other areas of government expenditure. For example, if health costs go up because of ageing, but education costs go down because of fewer students, then the net impact on the government would be less than the increase in health costs alone would suggest.

What effect will demographic ageing have on the economy? The most simple and truthful answer would probably be that no one knows.

If there are fewer students, then it is possible that re-sources will be reduced proportionally and little will change in the education system. However, if instead the same resources were used on fewer children, then educational attainment may improve, there may be lower student to teacher ratios, or students may stay in school longer. None of these situations are certain to occur, and if they did then the drop in costs might not be as large as predicted, but if they do happen then what would be the effects on society? There is evidence from the United States that smaller class sizes leads to educational improvement, especially for younger students and traditionally disadvantaged students. Another study from the United States suggests that the longer students spend in school, the less likely they are to commit crime. Using a similar methodology, [S.] Machin, [O.] Marie, and [V.] Suncica have shown the same to be true for the UK (2010). These results are not completely conclusive, but it is not hard to imagine that there are some possible positive societal effects from better education, and better education may be more likely with fewer students.

Economy

Finally, what effect will demographic ageing have on the economy? The most simple and truthful answer would probably be that no one knows, but there are some key areas of research to highlight. In the short-run there are many factors that affect economic growth, but in the long-run there are primarily two factors: the rate of increase of productivity and the size of the labour force. The labour force depends on the size of the population and economic participation rates for any specific age and sex. Participation rates can change in the future, but for any particular population, today's age-specific participation rates can be applied forward to give an estimate of the future size of the labour force. The link between an ageing society and productivity growth is more uncertain. On the one hand, older workers may need less training and therefore could be more productive. On the other hand, they may be less mobile and slower. One study suggested that because there may be a shortage of labour in an older society, overall productivity may increase as a response. Overall the evidence from economists is inconclusive.

Society will certainly change some with an ageing population, and although not all of the connections are thoroughly understood, it is likely to put increased pressure on government expenditures. Furthermore, as people retire there may be shortages of labour in some areas.

Israel Faces a Disaster as Its Population Ages

Ronny Linder-Ganz

Ronny Linder-Ganz is an Israeli health reporter. In the following viewpoint, she reports that the Israeli Ministry of Health is concerned because of the poor quality of long-term care for the elderly in the country. Israel has a low public expenditure on the elderly, Linder-Ganz says, and this has resulted in poor public care and a strained private insurance market. The problem is likely to become significantly worse as Israel's population ages. Linder-Ganz concludes by pointing to a number of programs and initiatives that Israel is taking to attempt to confront this problem.

As you read, consider the following questions:

1. What does Dr. Roni Gamzu say people do when state health care is bad, and how does this affect the private insurance market?
2. What does the state want to do about at-home care, and how does it propose to pay for this change?
3. According to the central bank of Israel, how will expenditures on continuing care for the elderly increase in the future?

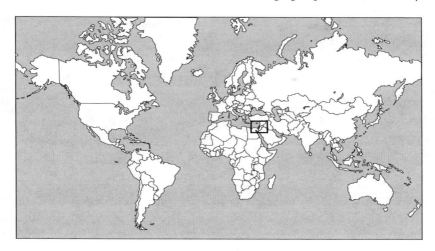

Health Ministry director general Dr. Roni Gamzu warned yesterday [March 19, 2012] that Israel faces a "horrendous crisis" in the next two decades in relation to the country's aging population, and that "the government must make the correct decisions on the matter."

The State Is Unprepared

Gamzu was responding to a report released Sunday by the Bank of Israel on the public services network for long-term care of the elderly in Israel.

The report highlights the worrying trend of an aging population and the poor quality of services for that population. The central bank's report is part of its annual report, which will be published in full at the end of the month.

Israel faces a "horrendous crisis" in the next two decades in relation to the country's aging population.

Israel's public expenditure on elderly citizens is among the lowest in the West, the Bank of Israel reported. The state isn't prepared to handle elderly citizens, and the problem will only get worse as the population ages, the report says.

"The service the state offers today for caring for the elderly in the community, and the lack of cooperation between the various bodies that handle the care for the elderly, have caused a systematic failure and the deterioration of many elderly until they have to be hospitalized," said Gamzu. He said it also causes very high private expenditures with a crazy level of private nursing care insurance for two-thirds of the population—which has led the entire insurance market for nursing care to high premiums and bankruptcy.

The state spends only NIS [Israel new shekel, the Israeli currency] 5.8 billion on elderly care a year, while private expenditures are higher than average, found the central bank. In total, NIS 9.9 billion is spent on care for the elderly every year—1.2% of GDP [gross domestic product]. The report also notes that because of bureaucracy, many senior citizens don't receive all they're entitled to.

The state isn't prepared to handle elderly citizens, and the problem will only get worse as the population ages.

"The number of elderly [aged over 65] in Israel, their proportion in the total population and the proportion in the population of the very elderly [aged over 80] have increased greatly since the 1970s, and are expected to continue rising rapidly in the future," wrote the Bank of Israel.

"The minute the public product is bad, everyone flees to the private market, usage increases and premiums rise," said Gamzu, referring to private insurance for elderly care. "What was sold in the past as a service at affordable prices for everyone, has turned into an expensive and problematic product," he added.

Systematic Failure

Gamzu said the ministry would soon try to pass the first stage of a reform proposed by Deputy Health Minister Yaakov Litz-

---

Long-Term Care Insurance Program

The Long-Term Care Insurance Program (LTCIP) in Israel is a social security program administered by the National Insurance Institute (NII) since 1988. LTCIP focuses on home-based personal care services. Differently from most other programs under the responsibility of the NII, LTCIP benefits are in-kind benefits and are delivered via multiple for-profit and not-for-profit organizations. In recent years LTCIP has been the target of various legal amendments and numerous administrative changes. While many of these changes may have had significant effects on individuals, they have not altered the fundamental principles of the program. Thus, many of the characteristics of beneficiaries have remained quite stable over the years; other characteristics of the population of beneficiaries have changed over the years reflecting the aging of Israeli society. A central issue related to LTCIP is whether benefits are adequate to meet the needs of the growing elderly population of Israel. While the generosity of LTCIP benefits is questionable, economic and political struggles have limited the scope of changes introduced thus far.

Sharon Asiskovitch,
"The Long-Term Care Insurance Program in Israel: Solidarity with the Elderly in a Changing Society,"
Israel Journal of Health Policy Research, *vol. 2, no. 3, January 23, 2013.*

---

man on care for the elderly. The plan would increase the number of weekly hours of at-home care paid for by the state from 18 to 30. The ministry feels the Bank of Israel has given its support for Litzman's reforms.

In addition, the ministry wants to take all the various care options run by different bodies and make the health funds responsible—and have the state-subsidized health basket pay for the care as part of the health tax, which would be increased by 0.5%.

This would guarantee care for the elderly in both the community and in nursing care for everyone. This is the opposite of the present situation, where the state provides only very partial support. Such state support for elderly care is also contingent on means tests for the family. In addition to adding caregiver hours at home, the ministry wants to provide funding for family members who take care of the elderly—and cancel most of the means tests.

"The higher proportion of elderly in the population is also reflected by an increase in the old-age dependency ratio, which is the ratio of the elderly population to the working-age population (20–64), and by an increase in the proportion of the over 65s who suffer from physical limitations which impair their ability to carry out day-to-day activities," the central bank said. The Health Ministry also wants to become the sole regulator and supervisor of elderly care.

The biggest opponent to the proposed reforms is the Finance Ministry, which objects to raising the health tax.

The National Insurance Institute [NII] has its own reform proposals, which do not involve granting the Health Ministry sole control over the matter. The NII's proposals, which were adopted in general by the Trajtenberg Committee on socioeconomic reform last year, include focusing budgets for elderly care mostly on those who are bedridden or needy. The cabinet has yet to discuss these proposals because of the Health Ministry's objections.

"In 2010, public expenditure on long-term care for the elderly amounted to NIS 5.8 billion, or 0.7% of GDP, and national (public and private) spending for this care reached NIS 9.9 billion, or 1.2% of GDP in that year. The ratio of this public expenditure to GDP in Israel is low in comparison to other OECD [Organisation for Economic Co-operation and

Development] countries, even taking into account the fact that the population in Israel is younger. In addition, the share of private spending on continuing care for the elderly in total expenditure on this item (public and private) is higher than in OECD countries. In Israel, demographic developments alone are expected to increase public expenditure on such care by at least 30% (at fixed prices) by 2019, and by more than 300% by 2059. This is assuming that the proportion of the elderly requiring continuing-care services among the age groups remains at its present level," wrote the central bank.

"In this respect, ways must be found to enhance the coordination between the different services in the community and in institutions, and to increase the efficiency of the means tests in a manner that will improve public services to the elderly and their families, and that will help them to fully exercise their rights. The reforms proposed in the area of caregiving should be focused on planning a suitable structure for public services for the elderly, in the community and in institutions, and on the manner in which they are to be financed in accordance with forecast demographic developments," wrote the Bank of Israel.

Worldwide, the Aging Population Can Create Opportunities

Julika Erfurt, Athena Peppes, and Mark Purdy

Julika Erfurt is a manager in Accenture's strategy practice; Athena Peppes is a senior research specialist at Accenture; and Mark Purdy is Accenture's chief economist and a senior executive research fellow. In the following viewpoint, the authors argue that populations are aging, in both the developed and developing worlds. They say that this presents many opportunities, since older people are more productive and spend more money than younger workers and consumers. If governments prepare, population aging need not reduce employment or burden pension systems, they say, but could instead create economic opportunities and growth.

As you read, consider the following questions:

1. What statistics do the authors provide to show that countries in the developed world are aging?
2. What is the "lump of labor fallacy," and why is it incorrect according to the authors?

Julika Erfurt, Athena Peppes & Mark Purdy, "The Seven Myths of Population Aging: How Companies and Governments Can Turn the 'Silver Economy' into an Advantage," Accenture Institute for High Performance, March 5, 2012. Copyright © 2012 by Accenture. All rights reserved. Reproduced by permission.

3. What do the authors say research has found about the relationship between entrepreneurship and age?

From Asia to the Americas, populations are getting older—a trend that is likely to continue for decades to come. So far, however, while perhaps acknowledging the existence of this trend, policy makers and business leaders have done little to prepare for it. In many cases, this inaction stems from misconceptions about older workers and consumers. We have identified seven common myths surrounding aging populations and highlight how organizations can find growth where others see only cost and limitations.

Dispelling Myths, Spurring Growth

"We're none of us getting any younger," the saying goes, and it's as true today as ever. What's different today, however, is that the global population isn't getting any younger either. In fact, because people are living longer and having fewer children, it's aging rapidly. Whereas today the global population aged 60 or over numbers nearly 750 million (more than 10 percent of the overall population), by 2050 it's expected to soar to more than 2 billion (perhaps exceeding 20 percent of the overall population). Of the forces that will shape society and the global economy over the next decades, none is more certain and predictable than population aging. In China and Japan this has led to inverted family pyramids, also called "four, two, one" in reference to four grandparents, two parents, and one child.

Despite the likelihood that the planet's population will steadily become much older over the next four decades, many business leaders and policy makers don't have a good grasp of the realities of population aging. In our conversations with leaders in both government and business, we frequently encounter misconceptions about the topic. These misconceptions have arisen from various sources. Some are the product of erroneous conventional wisdom, some are rooted in outdated assumptions and perceptions, and others overlook the extent to which policies and actions can address the aging trend.

Here we examine seven of these misconceptions, or "myths," and set the record straight for each. Our objective is not only to dispel these myths, but also to illustrate how companies and governments can spur growth and capture economic opportunities by crafting the right response to population aging.

Of the forces that will shape society and the global economy over the next decades, none is more certain and predictable than population aging.

Myth #1: Emerging economies will balance out the 'silver tsunami' of developed economies.

Reality #1: Population aging is a global trend that affects many emerging economies.

It's widely recognized that the populations of developed economies are aging. In Japan, more than 30 percent of the population is already aged 60 or over, a proportion that is steadily rising. The United Kingdom now has more people aged 60 or over than aged 16 or under. Business leaders and policy makers understand that this trend stems from declining birthrates and a dramatic increase in life expectancy.

However, many mistakenly believe that the populations of emerging economies are immune to this trend, and that their large, younger populations will be the salvation of the global economy. Goldman Sachs stresses that "young populations and rapidly expanding domestic markets" will turn the BRIC [Brazil, Russia, India and China] countries into four of the six largest economies by 2030.

In reality, however, the populations of emerging economies, such as China, Brazil and Mexico, are also getting older at a comparable pace. In 2010, those aged 60 and over represented 12 percent of the population in China, 10 percent in Brazil, and 9 percent in Mexico. By 2050, these figures are expected to increase to 31 percent, 29 percent and 28 percent, respectively.

Even countries with relatively youthful populations appear to be unable to avoid a similar fate. For example, Iran is experiencing the world's most rapid decline in birthrates—from a high of nearly 2 million births per year between 1985 and 1990 to a current level of around 1.2 million births and a projection of 700,000 births by 2050. South Korea currently has one of the youngest populations among OECD [Organisation for Economic Co-operation and Development] countries, but will become the second oldest by 2050.

Many mistakenly believe that the populations of emerging economies are immune to this trend, and that their large, younger populations will be the salvation of the global economy.

Of course, there are some countries whose populations will remain relatively young. For example, in India and South Africa nearly half the population today is under 25 years old. But even in those cases, considerable investment will be needed to convert raw numbers of young people into an employable and productive workforce that can be mobilized for future economic advantage.

Business leaders and policy makers in the developed economies should not expect that relatively younger populations in emerging economies will provide an automatic customer base or workforce to replace their aging counterparts in developed economies. And leaders in emerging economies must also find ways to sustain the employability and productivity of their aging populations.

Aging Is Not a Disaster

Myth #2: Countries with aging populations face decades of low growth.

Reality #2: By taking steps to increase the employment of older workers, countries can avert economic stagnation.

Commentators have been sounding alarms about the dire consequences of an aging population for a long time. According to these commentators, population aging will inevitably result in economic stagnation at best and decline at worst.

The scenario is indeed an alarming one. Aging populations increase the financial burden on governments, creating a pension time bomb and increasing demands on health care and elder care systems. As more people enter retirement, a vicious cycle of lower growth and higher taxes will arise. With fewer people in the workforce, disposable incomes will fall, reducing consumer spending.

By increasing the number of older people in the workforce and making productivity-enhancing investments in human capital, governments and businesses could boost economic growth and job creation.

In reality, this outcome is not inevitable. Leaders in both the public and private sectors can help their economies avoid this fate by taking steps to harness the productive potential of people who are living healthier lives, not just longer ones. In practice, this means addressing the incentives and systems that prevent older people from staying in the workforce, such as early retirement provisions, or pensions and tax systems that penalize people who work later in life. In 2006, the UK [United Kingdom] government introduced tough age discrimination laws, and in 2011 went one step further to completely abolish the default retirement age of 65. The UK's employment relations minister, Ed Davey, explained in support of the move that "retirement should be a matter of choice not compulsion."

We see significant opportunities to increase the time that people spend in productive employment. The OECD average for estimated years in retirement is 21 to 28 years for women and 14 to 24 years for men. A UK government study released in 2011 found that increasing time in the workforce by just one year per person would boost the level of real GDP [gross domestic product] by approximately 1 percent.

Our research at Accenture, in collaboration with Oxford Economics, shows that by increasing the number of older people in the workforce and making productivity-enhancing investments in human capital, governments and businesses could boost economic growth and job creation. We estimate that the United States could increase its GDP by $442 billion and lift employment levels by 5 million by 2020.

In Germany, similar measures to harness the "silver economy" have the potential to boost GDP by €61 billion and lift employment levels by 1.5 million by 2020. The research uncovered a similar story in the United Kingdom and Spain.

Myth #3: Employment is a zero-sum game, so retaining older workers will only worsen the crisis of youth unemployment.

Reality #3: Retaining older workers is likely to increase overall employment growth.

Unemployment is reaching record levels, particularly among the young. In December 2011, the UK crossed the threshold of one million unemployed young people, while in Spain approximately 52 percent of 15- to 24-year-olds are unemployed. With so many young people struggling to gain a foothold in the workforce, many observers believe that retaining older workers will simply worsen the crisis. This view, dubbed "the lump of labor fallacy" by economists, assumes that the number of jobs in an economy is fixed, which in turn results in a misguided focus on protecting existing jobs.

The US National Bureau of Economic Research has found little evidence that older workers take jobs away from younger ones in the United States. In some cases, such as in France and Canada, the researchers also found that greater workforce participation among older people was associated with greater participation among young people, because of the increase in the overall economic pie. Civic Ventures' "Encore" program is a powerful example of offering second careers to older HP [Hewlett Packard] and Intel executives in the nonprofit sector.

To spur overall economic growth, business leaders and policy makers should devise incentives and training programs that will enable older workers to stay in the workforce, rather than push them out to make room for younger workers.

No Decline with Age

Myth #4: Older workers tend to be less productive.

Reality #4: Organizations can sustain older workers' productivity by adapting the workplace to their needs.

The myth is contained in this scenario: An organization primarily employs people aged 50 and over, having long tenure. While they are competent and knowledgeable, many are reluctant to embrace new ideas, are uncomfortable with making changes, aren't well motivated, and find early retirement increasingly enticing. Consequently, productivity is lower than in a workplace dominated by younger workers.

In reality, "productivity rises with age all the way up to retirement," according to a study of German production line workers in a Mercedes-Benz truck factory. The authors concluded that although deteriorating physical ability meant older employees made more minor mistakes, these were "outweighed by the positive effects, such as the ability to cope when things go wrong."

Emerging Markets: Getting Older, Too

In three of the leading high-growth emerging markets, the percentage share of the total population over the age of 60 is trending rapidly upward; in parallel, the percentage of those under 15 is shrinking. Developed economies can't depend on youthful populations in emerging economies to bail them out by keeping productivity and output high.

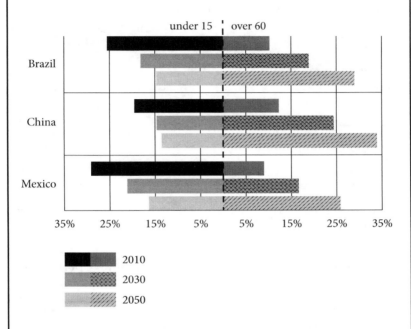

TAKEN FROM: Julika Erfurt, Athena Peppes, and Mark Purdy, "The Seven Myths of Population Aging: How Companies and Governments Can Turn the 'Silver Economy' into an Advantage," Accenture, March 5, 2012.

A recent Swedish study examined productivity in nearly 9,000 manufacturing plants. Controlling for plant-level effects, the researchers found that plants with a high proportion of older adults were more likely to have higher productivity than were plants with a high proportion of young people.

By adopting new work models, organizations can engage people who aren't able or interested to work full-time. Small adjustments in the physical environment can address changes in employees' physical strength and stamina, which tend to decline with age.

[Car manufacturer] BMW, for example, implemented 70 changes to a production line where the (older) employee profile reflected the company's expected overall workforce profile in 2017. The changes covered health care management and skills enhancement, as well as improvements to the workplace environment, such as orthopedic footwear and adjustable work tables. The production line's productivity improved 7 percent in one year, bringing it to the same level as lines staffed by younger workers.

"Productivity rises with age all the way up to retirement."

Also, the deployment of technology and new work models enable flexible and remote work arrangements that might be more appealing to older workers. MITRE Corporation, a US research and development enterprise, was concerned about losing its expertise in fields such as radar. It launched the "Reserves at the Ready" program to bring back retirees on a part-time, on-call basis.

Myth #5: The entrepreneurial spirit tends to decline with age.

Reality #5: Older people are more likely to set up a new business, and they're less likely to fail.

Setting up a new business is normally considered the preserve of the young. Witness the wave of young technology-company founders consistently featured on magazine covers. Governments tend to focus their entrepreneurship policies and objectives on the young. New funds are set up to help young entrepreneurs, such as the "20 Under 20" Thiel Fellowship announced in 2011. There have even been claims that for some sectors, like technology, the peak age for entrepreneur-ship is similar to that for top athletes, at 25 years old.

But recent research has found that age is not the pre-eminent factor influencing entrepreneurship, and that factors such as educational background and professional networks are more likely to play a role. In fact, many people decide to set up a business in later life. In the United Kingdom, entrepreneurs aged 50 to 65 created 27 percent of successful start-up companies between 2001 and 2005, equivalent to 93,500 companies. During that period, this age group accounted for 18 percent of the UK population.

A recent survey in Finland of 839 small firms established in the country between 2000 and 2006, found that 16 percent were set up by those aged 50 to 64. And in the United States between 2005 and 2010, entrepreneurial activity among those aged 45 and above increased during the recession, while it declined among the 18- to 44-year-olds.

Older people are also more likely to succeed in their new business ventures, with surveys finding that ventures started by those aged 50 and over had the lowest failure rates. Entrepreneurship among older people could potentially be even higher if age-related barriers were removed. For instance, access to seed capital and funding is crucial in setting up a new business. Yet many older people confront age limits for financial products and higher interest rates for loans, or are excluded from insurance products.

Marketing and Technology

Myth #6: Older consumers are an unattractive demographic for marketers.

Reality #6: Older consumers have vast purchasing power, making them an untapped opportunity for marketers.

Many marketers don't get excited about targeting products to older consumers. They aren't big spenders, the argument goes, because they have less disposable income and often prefer to keep money in the bank rather than spend it. What's more, they're less mobile and have established brand preferences, so it's harder to convince them to try new products, the skeptics believe.

Research reveals that these skeptics hold sway. A recent survey found that only 37 percent of companies find it fairly important to take into account the needs and preferences of older consumers when developing products for them. Most companies take great care in distinguishing between 20- or 40-year-olds, but lump 50- and 70-year-olds into the same category. This skepticism is also reflected in marketing practices, as research shows that only about 30 percent of TV advertisements include someone over 50. Not surprisingly, 70 percent of people over 55 believe that advertising does not speak to their needs.

In reality, what the skeptics fail to understand is that older consumers have vast purchasing power. In the United States, consumers aged 50 and above outspent younger adults by approximately $1 trillion in 2010. In the same year, baby boomers in the US were reportedly the dominant spenders in 1,023 out of 1,083 consumer packaged goods categories. In the United Kingdom, baby boomers hold around 80 percent of all financial assets. In Europe, the over-65 age group is estimated to be worth more than €300 billion.

Clearly, companies have not invested sufficient time, money and resources in understanding the untapped opportunity offered by older consumers. Companies should start by adopting more inclusive product development strategies and marketing approaches that include consumers of all ages. Some companies have already expanded their product range to cater to older consumers. For example, Harley-Davidson—recognizing that the average age of its customer has increased from 38 to 46 years old in the last two decades—is designing new motorcycles to appeal to consumers in their sixties and beyond.

Marketing for silver consumers however has to fit hand in glove with brand perception. A good example is Unilever's Dove soap campaign that featured women from everyday life and captions like "Why aren't women glad to be gray?" The campaign helped the company substantially boost sales around the world—no mean feat for the static soap category.

What the skeptics fail to understand is that older consumers have vast purchasing power.

Myth #7: Older consumers are less likely to adopt new technology.

Reality #7: The digital divide isn't inherently age based, and it will close over time.

There is a common misperception that older people are slow to engage with new technologies. Older people can't keep up with the latest technological developments, and aren't early adopters or trendsetters. You can't teach an old dog new tricks, these skeptics believe.

Research shows that although this might have been true in the past, the story is now changing. It's true that there is a digital divide between the old and the young in many countries. In Germany, for instance, only 31 percent of those aged 65 and over used the Internet in 2010, compared with an average of more than 75 percent for the overall population.

But this is due to lack of experience rather than age—it reflects a generational difference rather than an inherent relationship between age and technology adoption. Many of the younger baby boomers were in the workforce during the evolution of computers, email and the Internet, and were the first to understand the value of technology.

In Germany, 75 percent of those aged 45 to 64 in 2010 regularly used the Internet, in line with figures for the overall population. Nearly 80 percent of US baby boomers use the Internet for social media, downloading music and movies, financial transactions and gaming. The tech-savvy middle-aged of today will comprise an equally tech-savvy cohort of seniors in the coming decades. One product that has managed to transcend age barriers is Apple's iPad: from design to marketing the product is age inclusive, contributing to its wide appeal. For example, the powerful zoom, intelligent keyboard and voice functions such as auto-text mean that it's very easy to use and accessible. Likewise, the advertising campaign shows people of all ages engaging with the product.

Discarding Myths, Realizing Opportunities

Both business leaders and policy makers must recognize that now is the time to address population aging. As a starting point, business leaders can assess their company's preparedness on key dimensions, by asking the following questions:

Have we quantified the opportunities arising from population aging?

Do we offer flexible, tailored work models that support the changing needs of older workers?

In Germany, 75 percent of those aged 45 to 64 in 2010 regularly used the Internet, in line with figures for the overall population.

Do we have programs and incentives that encourage the exchange of knowledge between generations?

Do we have detailed customer profiles and market intelligence on consumers aged 55 and over?

Do we have an innovation strategy focused on the needs and preferences of older consumers?

Policy makers can make a start by focusing on the following questions:

- Does our education policy include a strategy for supporting lifetime skill formation?

- Are tax and pension systems aligned to encourage older people to stay in the workforce?

- Do our digital policies sufficiently address the needs of an aging population?

- Are we stimulating and leading discussions among researchers, business leaders and policy makers on the issues arising from an aging population?

- Are we addressing the barriers—such as access to capital, or regulation—that frequently stymie the entrepreneurial potential of the older population?

"Demography is destiny," the sociologist Auguste Comte stated almost two hundred years ago. This may well be true, but that destiny is not immutable. Just as aging individuals must adjust lifestyles to maintain personal vitality, societies with aging populations must adjust business practices and policies to boost their economic vigor.

In Japan, Aging Women Face Economic Hardships

Suvendrini Kakuchi

Suvendrini Kakuchi is a Sri Lankan journalist based in Japan; she has been covering Japan-Asia relations for more than two decades. In the following viewpoint, she reports that women are living longer lives in Japan and that this creates serious economic difficulties. Most women in Japan, Kakuchi says, give up work to look after their families and raise children. As a result, their earnings are less than men, and they have less money on which to retire. Kakuchi concludes that Japan and other nations need to do more to address the particular difficulties of elderly women.

As you read, consider the following questions:

1. According to Kakuchi, how has Hiroko Taguchi managed to avoid the poverty of many aging women in Japan?
2. What is women's life expectancy compared to men's in Japan?
3. What dangers do older Japanese women increasingly face, according to Junko Fukazawa?

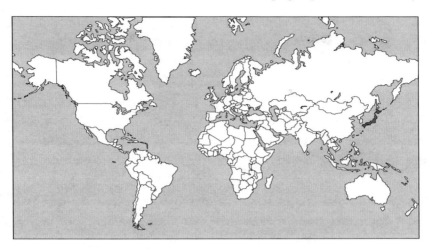

When Hiroko Taguchi retired this past April [in 2012], at the age of 64, from her job as an insurance sales agent, she joined the rapidly growing ranks of Japan's aging women who now outnumber their male counterparts.

Old Age and Poverty

Taguchi, a divorcee who lives alone, is heavily dependent on her pension to support what will likely be a lengthy retirement, given that women in Japan live, on average, about seven years longer than men. A survey conducted earlier this year by the Health[, Labour] and Welfare Ministry revealed that women account for 87.3 percent of Japan's record number of 50,000 centenarians.

"I am lucky I did not quit my job when I married, as was the norm for women of my age," Taguchi told IPS [Inter Press Service]. Indeed, she is one of a very small number of women in Japan for whom old age is not synonymous with poverty and loneliness.

Most of her contemporaries who were part-time workers or full-time homemakers in their youth and middle age now draw monthly public pensions of just 500 dollars or less—barely enough to cover their living costs.

A patriarchal social structure that has boxed women into the role of caretaker and homemaker is largely responsible for the vulnerable situation many old Japanese women now find themselves in.

According to government data, 70 percent of women leave their jobs when they start a family, returning to the workplace—often as part-time workers—only when their children are older; this pattern significantly reduces their chances of drawing a decent pension after retirement.

Additionally, the fact that women are experiencing increasingly long life spans means that many outlive their husbands and become entirely reliant on the state welfare system.

A patriarchal social structure that has boxed women into the role of caretaker and homemaker is largely responsible for the vulnerable situation many old Japanese women now find themselves in.

Social experts here say Taguchi's sunset years provide a spotlight into the diverse issues that women in Japan's graying society face today.

"More women than men face poverty in their old age given their (life spans) and lower incomes," pointed out Professor Keiko Higuchi, an expert on aging populations at Tokyo Kasei University, as well as an advisor to the government on gender and policies that affect the elderly.

Aging in a Patriarchal Society

Japan currently has the world's fastest-aging society. Experts estimate that by 2025 more than 27 percent of the population will be over 65 years old.

If the present trends continue, experts predict that 40 percent of the senior population will be female: Women are clocking 86.5 years, compared to 79.6 years for men.

Women and Aging

Globally, women form the majority of older persons. Today, for every 100 women aged 60 or over worldwide, there are just 84 men. For every 100 women aged 80 or over, there are only 61 men. Men and women experience old age differently. Gender relations structure the entire life course, influencing access to resources and opportunities, with an impact that is both ongoing and cumulative.

In many situations, older women are usually more vulnerable to discrimination, including poor access to jobs and health care, subjection to abuse, denial of the right to own and inherit property, and lack of basic minimum income and social security. But older men, particularly after retirement, may also become vulnerable due to their weaker social support networks and can also be subject to abuse, particularly financial abuse. These differences have important implications for public policy and programme planning.

United Nations Population Fund (UNFPA),
"Ageing in the Twenty-First Century:
A Celebration and a Challenge," 2012, p. 4.

Higuchi, who is also a prominent women's rights activist, has lobbied the government long and hard to develop policies that meet the needs of elderly women.

Among the many issues that aging women face are loneliness, higher prospects of disability and growing poverty in a nation that is grappling with a huge public debt and threatening further cuts in social services and state welfare.

Official statistics from the Health[, Labour] and Welfare Ministry confirm this grim picture—government data shows that 80 percent of those over 65 years and living alone are women, mostly divorcees and widows.

Women also comprise 70 percent of the population in nursing homes, with poverty affecting 25 percent of the female population over 75 years compared to 20 percent among males.

The ministry also reported that in 2011 there were almost 420,000 women over the age of 65 who depended on welfare handouts, compared to 324,000 men.

According to the prominent Japanese feminist Junko Fukazawa, who counsels women facing domestic violence—a risk she says is increasingly common for older women living with their husbands or sons—deep-rooted gender discrimination makes women even more vulnerable to the troubles of the sunset years.

Social traditions that have forced women to take care of the family while men worked outside "is the prime reason why women give up their jobs when they have children, (and end up with) lower-paying jobs and financial instability in their old age", Fukazawa told IPS.

"The situation is ironic," she added, pointing out that those who have traditionally been the primary caregivers for young and old alike are now becoming a population that needs the most support.

Those who have traditionally been the primary caregivers for young and old alike are now becoming a population that needs the most support.

The critical need to focus national aging policies on women is gaining traction around the world. A new report, 'Ageing in the Twenty-First Century: [A Celebration and a Challenge]', released in September by the United Nations Population Fund (UNFPA), calls on governments and other stakeholders to take heed of the mounting body of evidence that women are living longer than men, and adjust their national plans accordingly.

The report documented figures around the world that showed that for every 100 women aged 80 years and over, there are only 61 men.

Aging in Japan, the world's third largest economy, illustrates some of these pressing issues against the backdrop of a shrinking working population, which is expected to plummet from 80 to 52 million by 2050.

For the younger generation of Japanese women, who are coming of age during a time of government austerity and desperate attempts to reduce public spending, the forecast is alarming.

Already this generation of women is beginning to feel the crunch of poverty, with labour department statistics pointing to a rise in lower-paid part-time female employment, a trend that indicates an erosion of retirement stability for a large portion of the labour force.

For Higuchi, "The current aging picture clearly shows that Japan's economic growth policies have eroded traditional family values that protected old people and have been particularly unfair to women."

Meanwhile, women like Taguchi are moving cautiously down the road. "Acutely aware that I would face a lonely future, I have saved for decades and will continue to do so. At least I can avoid poverty—I hope so, anyway."

In China, the One-Child Policy Has Created Difficulties for Elder Care

Lan Fang

Lan Fang is a staff reporter for Caixin Online. In the following viewpoint, she argues that China is facing a crisis in elderly care. The one-child policy, which reduces the number of children couples can have, means there are fewer young people to look after the elderly. In addition, Fang says, migration to cities by the young has left many elderly unable to rely on their adult children for support. The government has so far failed to pick up the slack. Fang concludes that, as China's economy improves, the country has a duty to provide adequate care for its elderly.

As you read, consider the following questions:

1. According to Fang, what are "empty nests" in China?
2. How does China compare in elderly care beds per 1,000 of population with developed countries?
3. How do average Chinese pensions compare with the average cost of Chinese nursing homes?

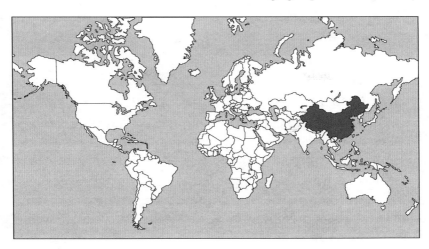

A 92-year-old nursing home resident in Beijing slumps in his wheelchair. Immobile and suffering from severe dementia, he requires daily care from nurses. Next to him, there are dozens more elderly patients sitting in wheelchairs, awaiting a scheduled activity or meal. These are the very fortunate. In cities across China, millions of elderly are facing a growing shortage of residential facilities and nursing services for senior citizens.

Too Many Elderly

In Beijing, all public nursing homes are currently filled to capacity, with waiting lists that fill up and spill over in greater volume from one year to the next. Beijing's 3,800 retirement homes and 60,000 beds can't meet the needs of the 2.3 million senior citizens. By the end of 2009, there were 167 million people over the age of 60 in China, approximately 12.5 percent of the nation's total population. Of these, 18.99 million were over the age of 80 and 9.4 million were disabled.

Current social safety nets cannot accommodate the situation.

"A disabled senior citizen places a burden on the entire family," said Yang Tuan, deputy director of the Social Policies Research Centre from the Chinese Academy of Social Sciences.

In cities across China, millions of elderly are facing a growing shortage of residential facilities and nursing services for senior citizens.

Moreover, with family sizes decreasing over the years, and empty nests—aging parents separated from children who migrated to cities—becoming more common, traditional family support is overburdened.

In the views of many social scholars, a substantial increase in investment for elderly care infrastructure and services is an urgent priority. This year [2010], for the first time, the establishment of a basic elderly care system was included in China's 12th Five-Year Plan, although experts have already begun to deride the system's feasibility on poor statistics.

The Shrinking Circle

The change in family demography is a major reason behind the growing need for elder care. China has adopted the one-child policy for 30 years. Parents of first generation only children are in their later years now. One couple caring for four elders and one child is becoming common, meaning the family burden has become very heavy for each young person.

Meanwhile, urbanization, migration and smaller families place additional pressures on the multigenerational upbringing function of the family. There are 49.7 percent "empty nests" among urban seniors. Growing "empty nest" families and decreasing family size greatly reduce the families' support for the elderly. Unfortunately, some senior citizens suffer from abandonment.

Internationally, elderly care institutions in developed countries have 50 to 70 beds for every 1,000 people. In China, there are 23.5 beds for every 1,000 people over the age of 65. This makes for bed shortage amounting to roughly 3 million. Professional nurses are in even greater shortage. There are only around 200,000 nurses in the entire country for senior care and only one-tenth of them have nursing licenses.

In traditional Chinese society, the family carries the burden of elderly care, but several factors have eroded this structure. The families now have to rely on social institutions and services, which exacerbates the problem.

Li Baoku, president of the China Ageing Development Foundation, said, "The suicide rate among the elderly in rural areas of China is four to five times higher than the world average. Many elderly choose to quietly finish their days in these cabins on a barren hillside, forest or stream, in order to avoid becoming a burden to their children."

Many elderly choose to quietly finish their days in these cabins on a barren hillside, forest or stream, in order to avoid becoming a burden to their children.

Beyond Material Necessities

With the lack of family care, as well as the weakening of the family support function, the need for external social support has become urgent. Most senior citizens can't afford the monthly costs of 2,000 to 3,000 yuan at a nursing home. The national average retirement pension is about 1,200 yuan per month. In rural areas, 90 percent of the elderly have no retirement pension at all. Due to gaps in the current pension system, nearly 70 percent of senior citizens rely primarily on their children and grandchildren for economic support.

A scholar at the Chinese Academy of Social Sciences, Sun Bingyao, says that the demand for elderly services has grown with the increase in the average life span. However, "The design of our elderly care system is concerned with the basic material life. We didn't take the care services into consideration."

Sun further explained that the impoverished conditions of China's senior citizens imply that the effective demand in China's elderly care market is insufficient, resulting in slow development in this market. Many lower- and middle-income families face the dilemma of high-quality care being out of their financial grasp, the limited places in nursing homes and possible maltreatment of elderly in nursing homes.

The government should bear the responsibility as the last line of defense, if the market and the third party can't provide services for the elderly, said Yan Qingchun, deputy director of the China National Committee [on Ageing].

Many scholars believe that the government's policy on social welfare has been incoherent as the economy continues to develop, making it impossible to provide unaffordable social services to those in need as a "socialist state." There is a lagging political impetus to stimulate supply from third parties such as NGOs [nongovernmental organizations] or private nursing homes.

"China's per capita GDP has already passed the US $3,000 mark—it's a middle-income country," said Wang Zhenyao, the head of the [China Philanthropy] Research Institute at Beijing Normal University and a former official at the Ministry of Civil Affairs. With greater economic development, Wang said the country has a duty to find a solution for elderly care by increasing investment in social welfare services.

Periodical and Internet Sources Bibliography

The following articles have been selected to supplement the diverse views presented in this chapter.

Joel Achenbach	"World Population Not Only Grows, But Grows Old," *Washington Post*, October 30, 2011.
Gavin Blair	"How Japan's Fukushima Disaster May Exacerbate Population Woes," *Christian Science Monitor*, August 11, 2011.
Economist	"Demography: China's Achilles Heel," April 21, 2012.
European Commission	"Greying Europe—We Need to Prepare Now," May 15, 2012. http://ec.europa.eu/news /economy/120515_en.htm.
Amanda Gardner	"Aging Population Poses Long-Term Challenges to U.S. Economy," *U.S. News & World Report*, September 25, 2012.
Guardian	"How Can We Prepare for an Ageing Population?," December 21, 2012.
International Labour Organization	"Ageing Societies: The Benefits, and the Costs, of Living Longer," December 1, 2009. http://www.ilo.org/global/publications /magazines-and-journals/world-of-work -magazine/articles/WCM_041965/lang--en /index.htm.
Slate	"China May Ease One-Child Policy in 2013," November 28, 2012.
Spengler	"Israel, Ireland and the Peace of the Aging," *Asia Times*, June 7, 2011.
The Wisdom Years	"Ageing Societies." http://wisdom.unu.edu /en/ageing-societies.

Policy Solutions to Aging Populations

Brazil Can Solve Infrastructure Problems Associated with Its Aging Population

Michael W. Hodin

Michael W. Hodin is the executive director of the Global Coalition on Aging. In the following viewpoint, he argues that Brazil has an opportunity to update its infrastructure to make the city friendly to and navigable by the aging and elderly. Hodin says that Brazil will be making numerous changes and improvements as it prepares to host the World Cup soccer championships in 2014 and the Summer Olympics in 2016. He argues that since Brazil's population is rapidly aging, age-friendly development could increase well-being and economic development. He says it could also lead the way for other nations whose populations are also aging.

As you read, consider the following questions:

1. How many people are turning sixty within the next decade, according to Hodin?

2. What support services does the *New York Times* say are missing in the favelas?

3. What factors are emphasized in the World Health Organization's age-friendly city guidelines?

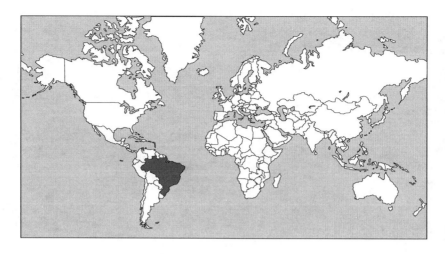

The London Olympics have come to an end, and the next must-see global sporting event won't occur until 2014, when the World Cup [the international soccer championship] kicks off in Rio de Janeiro. The Brazilians, one can only imagine, have already begun daydreaming about the glory of winning their sixth World Cup on native soil. But for all the premature fantasies and finger-crossing, Brazil must first deal with the business at hand: getting Rio ready not only for the continent's first World Cup, but also the soon-to-follow Summer Olympics of 2016.

Sport and Aging

As Brazil's public and private sectors coordinate to improve Rio's infrastructure, the country has the auspicious opportunity to both meet short-term spectator needs and solve long-term infrastructure issues associated with its ballooning aging population. Sport and aging may seem like an odd marriage, but there's an undeniable connection. The World Cup and the Olympics, most essentially, celebrate and promote health, activity and physical excellence. And as the population of Brazil and the rest of the world ages at an unprecedented rate, aging, too, becomes a celebration of health and activity. With two billion of us around the world turning 60 within a few decades, aging in the twenty-first century must become a time of continued physical and mental accomplishment.

A number of cities have begun to realize that urban infrastructure can become an enabling force for healthy, active aging. Taipei, Qiqihar, Newcastle upon Tyne and New York City, among others, have begun developing local projects that enable older people to remain active in social and economic life. Experts have argued that these infrastructure initiatives have tremendous benefits for mental and cognitive health. As the Brazilians pour billions into Rio, they would be wise to rebuild their city to meet the needs of their older population long after the world turns its attention elsewhere.

Brazil could create one of the world's foremost age-friendly cities.

The need for age-friendly development in Brazil is urgent. In 2010, the over-60 demographic made up 10 percent of Brazil's population. By 2050, that will total 29 percent, while the median age of Brazilians will be 45. Due to tremendous increases in longevity and persistent drops in fertility, the Brazilians are following in the footsteps of today's "oldest" countries such as Japan, South Korea, Germany, and others.

The chorus has been loud, of course, for Brazil to be smart and strategic about its infrastructure investments in Rio. A recent *New York Times* article pleaded, "In preparing for the World Cup and the Olympics, Rio has an opportunity to make long-term investments and integrate the favelas [Brazilian shanty towns] by providing the missing support services like education, job training, health care, day care, and sanitation." While this request makes good sense, it is incomplete. It misses the critical role of aging populations in long-term economic success in Brazil.

Characteristics of Age-Friendly Cities

Somewhere to rest

The availability of seating areas is generally viewed as a necessary urban feature for older people: It is difficult for many older people to walk around their local area without somewhere to rest.

> There are very few seating areas . . . you get tired and need to sit down.
>> Older person, Melville

Older people and caregivers in Shanghai appreciate the relaxing rest areas in their city. In Melbourne, the redevelopment of outdoor seating areas is viewed positively. Yet there is some concern about encroachment into public seating areas by people or groups who are intimidating or who display antisocial behaviour. In Tuymazy, [Russia,] for example, it was requested that the public seating be removed for this very reason.

Age-friendly pavements

The condition of pavements has an obvious impact on the ability to walk in the local area. Pavements that are narrow, uneven, cracked, have high curbs, are congested or have obstructions present potential hazards and affect the ability of older people to walk around.

> I had a fall due to the pavement, I broke my shoulder.
>> Older person, Dundalk

Inadequate pavements are reported as an almost universal problem.

World Health Organization,
"Global Age-Friendly Cities: A Guide," 2007, p. 13.

No Greater Challenge

Indeed, in the coming decades, Brazil—and much of the rest of the world—will face no greater social, political and economic challenge than the aging of its population. And for Brazil, this challenge is intensified by the large portion of the aging who live in poverty. In mapping out its infrastructure strategy, Brazil would be wise to consider how aging populations—and the aging who live in the favelas—could contribute to the country's emerging economy. With 29 percent of its population old by 20th-century standards, a 21st-century approach to aging and development could further bolster Brazil's impressive economic growth.

But what would this age-friendly development look like? At its most basic, it would follow the World Health Organization's age-friendly cities guidance, which emphasizes "the importance for older peoples' access to public transport, outdoor spaces and buildings, as well as appropriate housing, community support, and health services." But it would also enable a life-course approach to healthy aging—one that would keep "old" Brazilians engaged in social and economic life.

By partnering with top universities and health professionals, Brazil could create one of the world's foremost age-friendly cities just at the time when it has the world's attention. If Rio becomes "age friendly," it would be a huge win not only for Brazil, but also for the rest of the world. No city will be more watched and scrutinized over the next few years than Rio, and age-friendly development would set the city of Carnival as a model for all the world to see.

Over the past few years, it has become nothing short of common sense that development should be "green" and "environmentally friendly." Now, it's time for Rio to show the world that "age-friendly" development is of equal importance. If you ask the bookies in Vegas, they'll tell you the odds are well in favor of the Brazilians taking the Rio World Cup. And as nice as that would be for Brazil, it is far more important for the country to keep their aging populations at the heart of their booming economy.

Iran Is Trying to Encourage Childbirths to Offset Its Aging Population

Farzaneh Roudi

Farzaneh Roudi is the program director for the Middle East and North Africa Region at the Population Reference Bureau. In the following viewpoint, she argues that Iran's new fertility policy probably will not have much success in increasing births. Roudi says that until recently Iran had promoted family planning through education and health care services. She says that rolling these programs back is difficult and unlikely, and the government's other initiatives are unlikely to have a major impact on increasing birthrates.

As you read, consider the following questions:

1. What statistics does Roudi provide to demonstrate Iran's success in lowering its fertility?
2. To what does Roudi attribute the success of Iran's family planning program?
3. What financial incentive has President Mahmoud Ahmadinejad provided to try to encourage families to have more children, according to Roudi?

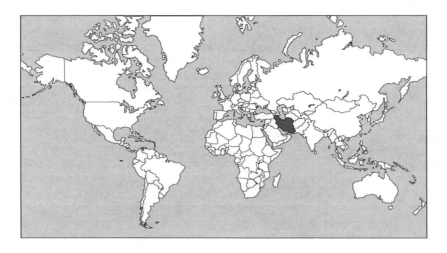

Once again, the Iranian government is reversing its population policy—its fertility policy, to be more precise. Alarmed by the country's rapidly aging population, Iran's supreme leader Ayatollah Ali Khamenei is now calling on women to procreate and have more children, and the Iranian Minister of Health and Medical Education Marzieh Vahid Dastjerdi has recently said, "The budget for the population control program has been fully eliminated and such a project no longer exists in the health ministry. The policy of population control does not exist as it did previously." This comes at a time when the government is barring women from entering some academic fields in higher education, which makes one wonder if this is a coordinated effort to engineer women's position at home and in society. Regardless, Iran's population control policy that came about more than two decades ago had increasingly become outdated for today's Iran.

Iran stands out for lowering its fertility in a short time without coercion or legal abortion. The total fertility rate dropped from 6.6 births per woman in 1977 to 2.0 births per woman in 2000 and to 1.9 births per woman in 2006. The decline has been particularly impressive in rural areas where the average number of births per woman dropped from 8.1 to 2.1

in one generation. (To put into perspective the speed at which Iran's fertility declined, it took about 300 years for European countries to experience a similar decline.)

Because of the high fertility rate that Iran experienced in the recent past, followed by a sharp decline, Iran's population is now aging rapidly. According to the United Nations Population Division, the median age in Iran increased from 18 in the mid-1970s to 28 today, and it is expected to increase to 40 by 2030 if the fertility trend continues. Yes, Iran is facing an aging population, and this may well be in the minds of Ayatollah Khamenei, President Mahmoud Ahmadinejad, and some other officials who are encouraging Iranian women to have more children.

History of the Population Policy and Family Planning Program

Iran has always been pragmatic toward its population policies and programs, and one would expect the same with their pronatalist initiative this time around as well. There have been three distinct periods in the history of Iran's family planning program, each marked by major changes in the government's population policy. A brief review of them can help us see what may come next.

Family Planning Before the 1979 Islamic Revolution. Iran was one of the first countries to establish a family planning program as part of its development plan. The Imperial Government of Iran launched its family planning program in the ministry of health in 1967. The program acknowledged family planning as a human right and emphasized its social and economic benefits for families and society. It recruited and trained a cadre of professional staff and taught many young doctors about family planning's implications for public health and its critical role in improving the well-being of women and children. Family planning became an integral part of maternal and child health services nationwide. By the mid-1970s, 37 percent of married women were practicing family planning, with 24 percent using modern methods. The total fertility rate, although declining, remained high at more than six births per woman.

The Islamic Revolution and Pronatalism. Days after the 1979 Islamic revolution, the family planning program was dismantled because it was associated with the Iranian royal family and was viewed as a Western innovation. The new government advocated population growth and adopted new social policies, including benefits such as allowances and food subsidies for larger families. In an attempt to ensure continued government support for family planning, however, a number of committed health professionals approached the government with information about the health benefits of family planning. They even obtained *fatwas* (religious edicts concerning daily life) from Ayatollah [Rouhollah Mousavi] Khomeini and other top-ranking clerics to the effect that "contraceptive use was not inconsistent with Islamic tenets as long as it did not jeopardize the health of the couple and was used with the informed consent of the husband." As a result, both government-sponsored and private-sector health facilities continued to provide family planning services as part of their primary health care. In 1980, Iran was attacked by Iraq. During the eight-year conflict that followed, having a large population was considered an advantage, and population growth became a major propaganda issue. Many Iranian officials were pleased when the 1986 census showed that Iran's population of close to 50 million was growing by more than 3 percent per year, one of the highest rates in the world.

Restoring the Family Planning Program. After the war with Iraq ended [in 1988], while focusing on drafting its first national development plan, the government saw rapid population growth as a major obstacle to the country's economic and social development and reversed its population policy, reviving the family planning program and promoting small family size. In 1993, the Iranian legislature passed a family planning bill that removed most of the economic incentives for large families. For example, some social benefits for children were provided for only a couple's first three children. The law also gave special attention to such goals as reducing infant mortality, promoting women's education and employment, and extending social security and retirement benefits to all parents so that they would not be motivated to have many children as a source of old age security. While all these legal reforms in support of the family planning program were significant and highlight Iran's commitment to slowing population growth, it is hard to assess their impact on lowering fertility.

In 1993, the Iranian legislature passed a family planning bill that removed most of the economic incentives for large families.

Why Iran's Family Planning Program Was Successful

The level and speed of the fertility decline was beyond any expectation. The first official target of the revitalized family planning program, as reflected in the government's first five-year development plan, was to reduce the total fertility to 4.0 births per woman by 2011. By 2000, the rate was already down to half of the stated goal.

The success of Iran's family planning program is largely attributed to the government information and education program and to a health care delivery system that was able to meet reproductive health needs. One of the many family planning posters produced by the Ministry of Health and Medical Education said, "Better life with fewer children; Girl or boy, two is enough." As part of promoting its notion of healthy, small families, the ministry of health established premarital

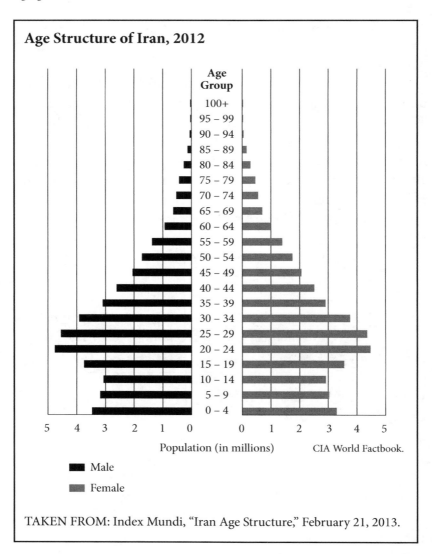

Age Structure of Iran, 2012

Age Group		
100+		
95 – 99		
90 – 94		
85 – 89		
80 – 84		
75 – 79		
70 – 74		
65 – 69		
60 – 64		
55 – 59		
50 – 54		
45 – 49		
40 – 44		
35 – 39		
30 – 34		
25 – 29		
20 – 24		
15 – 19		
10 – 14		
5 – 9		
0 – 4		

Population (in millions)   CIA World Factbook.

■ Male
■ Female

TAKEN FROM: Index Mundi, "Iran Age Structure," February 21, 2013.

counseling classes throughout the country; the government made it mandatory for couples planning to marry to participate before receiving their marriage license. Also, population education became part of the curriculum at all educational levels; university students, for example, had to take a course on population and family planning.

Family planning is one of many services provided for free by the country's primary health care system, which is based on different levels of care and an established referral system. That is why it is often referred to as a health care "network." Iran's primary health care system is recognized as a model by the World Health Organization (WHO). In rural areas, the Ministry of Health and Medical Education is the main provider of health care services, and health workers (*behvarz*) are proactive about reaching out to people. In urban areas, however, health services are largely provided by the private sector. Private health care and the pharmaceutical industry are relatively strong in Iran. Many modern contraceptives are manufactured in the country, making it largely self-sufficient—the only condom factory in the region is in Iran, which exports its products to neighboring and Eastern European countries. To encourage the use of its clinics in low-income areas in cities, the government uses women volunteers to connect people living in their neighborhood to a clinic and make appointments for them to receive basic services, such as immunizing children or receiving contraceptives. Today, the great majority (70 percent) of Iranians live in urban areas.

Now, Can the Government Roll All of This Back?

The answer is most probably not. The notion of small family size is now enshrined in the Iranian psyche, both men's and women's. They now have gotten used to exercising their reproductive rights and would expect to be able to continue to do so, whether it would be through government-sponsored health services or the private sector. Today, 74 percent of married women ages 15 to 49 practice family planning; 60 percent use a modern method; and one-third of modern contraceptive users have relied on a permanent method—female or male sterilization. These rates are more or less comparable to those in the United States.

73

Iranians have been progressive regarding their reproductive rights. Iranian women who have achieved their reproductive rights are at the forefront of the democracy movement in Iran, demanding even more rights. An overwhelming majority of Iranian women live a modern lifestyle that is often not seen in the Western media that show women covered head to toe in black, as if they belong to centuries ago. Elementary school enrollment is universal; the gender gap in secondary school enrollment is almost closed; and more girls have been enrolled in universities than boys (which prompted the government to set quotas for university entrants in favor of male students). Despite continued international economic sanctions and political isolation, secular ideas find their way into the country through satellite television and the Internet. Iranians have the second highest rate of Internet use in the Middle East and North Africa region, after the United Arab Emirates—although it should be noted that the Internet is filtered in Iran.

Today, Iranians' decision on whether to bring a child into this world is more complicated than just involving a financial incentive, such as the one that President Ahmadinejad introduced about two years ago and the ones that may follow to encourage families to have more children. Under Ahmadinejad's plan, each newborn receives a $950 deposit into a government bank account. They will then continue to receive $95 every year until they reach 18 years of age. Parents will also be expected to pay matching funds into the accounts. Then, children can withdraw the money at the age of 20 and use it for education, marriage, health, and housing. But Iranian parents, with their daily economic struggle to make ends meet, know that this amount is not going to go far, considering the high cost of living and skyrocketing inflation.

Bans Are Unlikely

It is unlikely that the Ministry of Health and Medical Education would ban family planning services altogether. Family planning is an important part of maternal and child health care. The Iranian constitution stipulates that the government is responsible for providing basic health care (including maternal and child health) and education to all of its citizens for free. So, one would expect family planning services to remain as part of a basic health care package. If not, then the government needs to deal with black markets selling contraceptives and the consequences of unwanted pregnancies, including abortion. Abortion is illegal in Iran, but it is practiced underground; because of that, they potentially are performed in unsanitary settings and by unskilled providers. Following WHO recommendations, however, the government does provide post-abortion care to treat complications resulting from unsafe abortions. In short, the human and financial resources of the Ministry of Health and Medical Education are better spent if they are used to provide family planning services to those who need them than used for dealing with the complications of unsafe abortions—not to mention loss of lives, as some women die as a result.

Regardless of what the government may or may not do, the number of births in Iran is going to increase for a decade or so.

It is also unlikely that the government would roll back its educational activities in schools or premarital counseling classes altogether. While these educational activities were originally developed for family planning purposes, over time they have been expanded to cover other reproductive issues, such as sexually transmitted diseases, including HIV. Iran has the largest number of people living with HIV/AIDS in the region.

It is not yet clear what schemes the government is going to use to encourage young people to marry in the first place and to have children soon after that. The government already has some programs in place that help young people with wedding expenses and provide appliances for their home—who supposedly otherwise could not afford them—but it is difficult to assess the impact of the program. More important, the number of those participating in the program is too small relative to the size of the country's young population—it can hardly have any impact on the national average age at marriage.

Births Will Increase

Welcomed schemes that may come about as the result of the new government initiative include free child care services across the country, longer maternity leave, and a higher level of child allowances for higher birth orders—schemes that some European countries experiencing low fertility rates have in place.

While these are all speculations, regardless of what the government may or may not do, the number of births in Iran is going to increase for a decade or so. Today, a significant portion of Iran's population is in its 20s and early 30s (prime ages to marry and have children), born during the high-fertility era around the 1979 Islamic revolution and the 1980s. So, the number of births is likely going to increase as these baby boomers go through their childbearing years. Therefore, one should not rush to judgment and attribute future increases in the number of births to the success of the Iranian government's pronatalist policies.

Rethinking Retirement in Korea Can Help Address an Aging Population

Chemin Rim

Chemin Rim is the minister of health and welfare of the Republic of Korea. In the following viewpoint, he says South Korea faces difficult economic and social choices due to its rapidly aging population. He suggests that the country should respond by providing seniors with opportunities to work and be productive longer, and by investing in policies to increase fertility by making child rearing less burdensome. He concludes that building cross-generational solidarity, so that people of different ages feel they are working together rather than against each other, is vital for South Korea's future.

As you read, consider the following questions:

1. What statistics does Rim provide about Korea's demographics in 2050?
2. How will Korea try to promote active aging for baby boomers, according to Rim?
3. What were the results of the OECD survey that asked if older people are a burden on society?

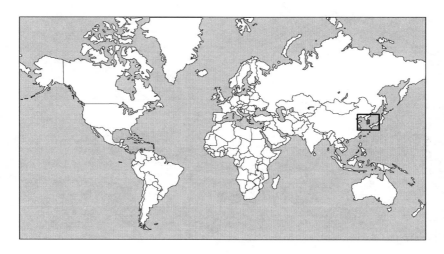

The world is struggling to find solutions to the problems of low fertility and aging. Korea is no exception. Aging is not simply a demographic transformation. It is closely linked with economic growth. It is an intergenerational solidarity issue as well. Our ultimate goal is threefold: good management of aging, fiscal sustainability, and continuous economic growth. However, it seems impossible to achieve the three goals at the same time. But there is a way ahead if we look at things from a different perspective.

"Demographic Time Bomb"

Korea has an ambitious plan to tackle the issue. We are trying to reverse the trend of low fertility with various incentives. We are also developing new engines of growth while making better use of untapped talents in our labor force. And we are working to help baby boomers prepare for their retirement and retirees to be more active. Korea is not the first country to attempt such action plans. And success is not guaranteed unless we change our attitude and way of doing business. Key to success seems to lie in the social consensus.

Economic sustainability is important. But intergenerational solidarity is even more important for a society to prosper.

Aging has some negative nicknames. "Demographic time bomb" is one, and "Age-quake" is another. They all capture the enormity of the challenge. Thus the world is preoccupied with finding solutions for the daunting challenges of low fertility and aging. Korea is on the edge of a precipice because its aging is the fastest in the world. With a fertility rate as low as 1.24, Korea is entering into an aged society in five years and a super-aged society in just 14.

This is not simply a demographic transformation. A society with many old people is not such a big problem in itself. We can provide them with necessary means of living in retirement and sufficient medical services. But things are not that simple. An aged or super-aged society is a potential catastrophe because it is necessarily linked with low birth so that there are fewer workers to support the elderly and sustain and grow the economy. Governments have to spend enormous amount of additional budget to finance the aged. Discontents emerge between generations. Younger generations complain about their growing burden for supporting over-the-hill generations.

Economic sustainability is important. But intergenerational solidarity is even more important for a society to prosper.

The Korean Case

Let me elaborate on the acute situation in Korea. When our government implemented birth control policies in the 1970s and 1980s, it would have been hard to imagine that Korea's fertility rate would fall to 1.24. Maybe the past policy was too successful. Now, Korea's fertility rate is only slightly over half the replacement rate of 2.1. If this trend continues, our population will peak in 2030 before starting a rapid decline. For the working-age population, the peak year is 2016—only three years away.

Everything in Korea seems to move fast. The proportion of elderly population tripled in a single generation; from 3.5 percent in 1975 to 11 percent in 2010. We are reaching a super-aged society with over 20 percent of old people in only 14 years from now. By 2050 the elderly population is projected to make up 37.4 percent, with more than half aged over 75. The old-age dependency ratio [that is, the ratio of those elderly not working to those working] will more than quadruple from 15.2 in 2010 to 71.0 in 2050. While it takes eight young people to support every old man now, the same burden should be borne by only two in 2050.

It is also a potential "demographic time bomb" on our economy. Expenditures in pension should rapidly increase from 0.9 percent of GDP [gross domestic product] in 2010 to 5.5 percent in 2050. The favorable demographic structure for the economy is coming to an end. The potential economic growth rate of current 4.6 percent is expected to be reduced to a mere 1.4 percent in 2050.

We have to do something, something big, and urgently. Maintaining the status quo is not an option. We have three goals to achieve at the same time: good management of aging, fiscal sustainability, and economic growth. We need to keep the economy rolling and provide social services for the elderly while maintaining fiscal balance. However, the current economic and social structure does not enable us to do so. We can currently achieve only two, not all three.

Everything in Korea seems to move fast. The proportion of elderly population tripled in a single generation; from 3.5 percent in 1975 to 11 percent in 2010.

To borrow a term from international economics, we are in a situation of "trilemma" or "impossible trinity." In economics, it is impossible to achieve a fixed exchange rate, free capital movement, and independent monetary policy at the same time. We can only pick two, not all three. Likewise in aging, unless things change, it seems to be impossible to achieve all three goals. We can manage aging and get economic growth, but not without detriment to budget balance. We can manage aging and sustain the fiscal health, but only without economic growth. And we can get economic growth and fiscal sustainability, but only with little or no service to the old people.

Then is there no way out? Fortunately, there is. Unlike the impossible trinity in international economics, we can surely escape from the aging trilemma. We can do it by changing the status quo, by changing the modus operandi of our economy, and by changing the attitude of people. But it is by no means easy. We will have to make some tough choices.

Korea's Plan to Tackle Low Fertility and Aging

We do have a plan. We made a law in 2005 . . . and established a presidential committee in the same year. Governmental action plans have been implemented since 2006. And we are now in the second phase of the "Basic Plan on Low Fertility and Aging Society 2011–2015." Naturally our goal is to increase the fertility rate and to successfully cope with the aging society. In order to achieve it, we have set three main tasks.

The first pillar is to create a favorable environment to raise the fertility rate. We are strengthening the system of child care leave and flexible working hours to help parents balance work and family. At the same time, we are ensuring that the burden will not be left only to families but shared by government, businesses and society by increasing public and private child care centers and awarding certification to family-friendly companies.

Second, we are trying to develop a new engine that will drive the economic growth against low fertility and aging through institutional adjustments to cope with demographic changes. We will make better use of untapped human resources including women and foreign workers. Socioeconomic systems of education, housing, finance and so on should be changed accordingly.

Third, we are working to help baby boomers prepare for their retirement. The government is making efforts to provide diverse employment opportunities, old-age income security, and preventive health management for them. Meanwhile, for the current elderly population, our efforts concentrate on the basic old-age pension, job creation, and the expansion of long-term care.

I will elaborate on the third pillar. Last July, the Korean government announced the action plans to create new opportunities for retiring baby boomers. "Active aging" or "productive aging" is the key word. They should be given opportunities to actively pursue meaningful lives. AARP's motto "to serve, not to be served" hits the mark.

First, we will delay retirement for as many working people as possible. The age ceiling in public institutions will be raised, and exclusive jobs for retirees are to be expanded and new ones created. Their initiative to business start-ups will be encouraged and relevant retraining will be provided. Second, we will support those who want to resettle in rural areas for agricultural activities with necessary information, customized training, and financial assistance. A large number of Koreans are thinking of "home-coming" to cultivate farms after retirement. Third, we will work to expand the programs where retiring baby boomers can volunteer to share their talent and expertise. They would find themselves valuable to the society.

The blueprint for baby boomers is an important, but only a partial, section of the whole picture. The supplementary measures to the "Basic Plan on Low Fertility and Aging Society 2011–2015", announced last October, encompass 62 core projects in five areas. They are designed to accomplish five essential values for aging and aged citizens: income security, continued health, social participation, comfortable housing and transportation, and smooth transfer to post-retirement.

The basic principle of the whole scheme may be summarized as "to serve, and to be served." Those who are able and willing to serve will be encouraged and supported to do so. Those who need to be served will be served. And those who like to serve but need to be helped to serve will be enabled and assisted accordingly.

First, we will delay retirement for as many working people as possible.

Intergenerational Solidarity Revisited

The OECD [Organisation for Economic Co-operation and Development] conducted an attitudinal survey for 21 members in 2009. It asked a provocative question: "Are older people a burden on society?" The results were interesting. Overall, only 14 percent of people answered yes. An absolute majority of 85 percent disagreed. More interestingly, people aged 40–50 who expect to retire soon strongly disagreed. But already retired old people tend to think of themselves as a burden. What about young people? They tend to think likewise.

Cross-country comparison shows that people are more likely to agree in countries where old people receive a high portion of incomes from the state. And interestingly again, intergenerational relations seem to be stronger where other sources play a more important role in old-age incomes. And intergenerational solidarity seems to be strongest when older people are seen to be helping themselves, either by continuing to work or by preparing private savings.

We do not have such surveys yet in Korea. But I presume that the OECD's findings may also apply to Korea as well. If we live longer, it may be inevitable for us to work longer. And if we work longer, there may be less tensions between the generations in the future. Are we really ready to work longer and postpone a work-free, always-holiday life? Are we really ready to get a reduced amount of pension? Even though we do want to work longer, is it acceptable to young people? Don't they think it is shrinking their job opportunities? Can it appeal as a popular choice for politicians and voters?

The answers are likely to be negative if we look at things from the current socioeconomic framework. Paying more tax for both babies-to-be-born and people soon-to-be-retired is by no means appealing to the working-age generation. The zero-sum game perception of jobs taken by elders as lost jobs for young people does not lead to any feasible solution for the entire society. If retirees insist on a high pension without being asked to work longer, the aging "trilemma" cannot be avoided. Sustainable economic growth under low fertility and aging is not possible if we continue to count only people between age 15 and 65 as the labor force population.

Are we really ready to get a reduced amount of pension? Even though we do want to work longer, is it acceptable to young people? Don't they think it is shrinking their job opportunities?

We have to make hard choices as well. Seniors should contribute to the economy as long as they can. They should be given chances to work if they want to. And they need to be more proactive and responsible to prepare for their own retirement. More importantly, a favorable environment must be created to reverse the trend of low fertility. Better child care services, more flexible working hours, and greater investment in education are likely to lead to higher short-term fiscal burden and higher taxes. But in the long run, all of these actions will pay off. And it seems to be the only option we have to escape the trap of an aging trilemma.

The Korean government's initiative to tackle the "age boom" covers all these aspects. Needless to say, ours is not the first attempt. We draw on experience and expertise from other forerunners in Scandinavian and other European countries. But socioeconomic institutions are difficult to transplant from one country to another. We may need to undergo a certain period of trial and error. What matters is how we can wisely shorten the transition.

What matters again is how we can sensibly persuade and mobilize the public for social consensus. Sustainable economic growth is important. But intergenerational solidarity is even more important for a society to keep existing and prospering while it ages.

Immigration Can Balance the Aging Population in Europe

Joan Muysken

Joan Muysken is a professor in the Department of Economics at Maastricht University in the Netherlands. In the following viewpoint, he argues that immigrants can benefit Europe. Specifically, immigrants will help European economies if the immigrants can find employment and if their distribution of skills is roughly in line with the distribution of skills within European countries. Muysken concludes that current European immigration policies, which favor high-skilled workers, are too restrictive, since Europe would also benefit from low-skilled workers who could find employment.

As you read, consider the following questions:

1. According to the viewpoint, what factors have ameliorated skill shortages in the United States?
2. Who does Muysken say the blue card program will attract?
3. What policies does Muysken recommend besides immigration to address skill shortages in Europe?

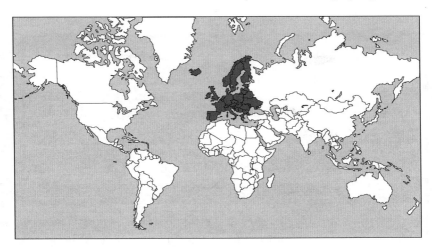

The European Union [EU] has recently adopted a new immigration policy, which includes the introduction of the "blue card", a European work permit similar to the American "green card". Apart from the treatment of highly skilled migrants, also the admission and procedures for seasonal workers, paid trainees and intra-corporate transferees will be regulated during the next few years. The new policy aims at solving skill shortages resulting from an ageing population. Eurostat predicts that the over-65 population will rise from 15.4% in 1995 to 22.4% by 2025, and the working-age population will shrink by over 50 million by 2050.

Immigrants and Skills

In this [viewpoint] we consider whether the new emphasis on skills is justified or not. Our analysis leads us to the conclusion that economic growth in the fast-aging EU will be sustained by immigration that enables EU countries to keep a balanced mix of skills in their labour markets.

According to [R.B.] Freeman (2006) immigration has been very important to tackle skill shortages in the US, even though the greying of the labour force is less severe than in Europe. His analysis shows that skill shortages caused by a rising de-

Changing Europe

From the varied discussions around the topic it is clear that in Europe there is a mounting population challenge that will lead to a shift in society. 'The low white birthrate in Europe, coupled with faster-multiplying migrants, will change fundamentally what we take to mean by European culture and society,' is one pertinent view. Many increasingly see that, to sustain competitive growth in the face of declining fertility, Europe will support increased migration—and this will largely come from North Africa and the Near East. Although raw data is highly sensitive and hard to come by, leading commentators see that, by 2020, economic migration will have started to change the multicultural balance in a new direction. Europe will become increasingly Muslim and, if current trends continue, over 10% of European nationals will be Muslim by the end of the decade.

Tim Jones, Future Agenda: The World in 2020.
Oxford, United Kingdom: Infinite Ideas Limited, 2011, p. 171.

mand for highly skilled workers are ameliorated by both an increase in the proportion of well-educated workers in US multinational firms outside the US, and a large inflow of foreign scientists and engineers. These developments have been made possible by the spread of mass education in many low-wage countries. . . .

Immigrants and Employment

Although the blue card seems to be a good instrument to attract more higher-educated individuals, we show that it may be beneficial for the European Union to attract also immigrants who have not graduated from universities as long as the skill distribution of the immigrants is on average not below that of the EU countries. It is, however, very important that immigrants are in paid employment, so that the goods and services they produce can be consumed by the growing share of the population that has retired.

Also the skill level of immigrants should be of second importance as long as they work, since low-skilled working immigrants can pay for the pensions of the retired people as well as the benefits of the unemployed native workers. Jobs for these immigrants can be available in for example construction, cleaning, security, personal care and domestic activities. Therefore the immigration policy of the European Union regarding the blue card, even when it is extended to regulate the admission of, for example, seasonal workers, may be too restrictive to maximise the benefits from immigration in the light of an ageing population. We show that the benefits from immigration could proliferate further if policy makers focus on an increase of the ratio of the working to the inactive population in general. . . .

Immigration should not be regarded as the sole cure for falling birthrates and ageing population.

Immigration and Unemployment

The main conclusion from our analysis is that income per capita will increase due to immigration, under the condition that the rate of unemployment does not increase. The highly skilled workers will profit anyway from the usual low-skilled immigration, and there may be important distributional effects for the low-skilled and the retired. The increase in capital accumulation following immigration turns out to be an important determinant of economic growth when analysing the benefits of immigration.

Our empirical analysis for the Netherlands reveals that there are at least two conditions that must be satisfied in order to get a positive impact of immigration on the economy. First, immigrants should get employed to stimulate economic growth. Second, the proportion of low-skilled immigrants in the total number of immigrants should not be higher than the proportion among natives to prevent unemployment from rising. Thus to stimulate investments and economic growth it is of utmost importance that immigration policy as a means to mitigate the aging problem should not only focus on the number of immigrants, but also on their employability by keeping the skill structure in line with the skill distribution of domestic labour market entrants. This requires two steps: (1) skill-neutral screening of immigrants and (2) an education policy that has the aim and ability to educate the second and third generations of immigrants, at least in line with the average skill distribution in a country.

Our conclusions support the view of the European Commission that immigrants in general have a positive impact on the economy provided that they are employed. As the European Commission puts it: "the current situation and prospects of EU labour markets can be broadly described as a 'need' scenario. Some member states already experience substantial labour and skills shortages in certain sectors of the economy, which cannot be filled within the national labour markets. This phenomenon concerns the full range of qualifications— from unskilled workers to top academic professionals." In line with this statement by the European Commission we argue that the immigration policy of the European Union with respect to the blue card and the admission of some other specific groups are too restrictive and do not maximise the benefits from immigration in the light of an ageing population.

Finally, immigration should not be regarded as the sole cure for falling birthrates and ageing population, since it is only one policy instrument within a broader mix of instruments. Immigration policies should go hand in hand with active labour market policies and education policies to get the low-skilled unemployed back to work and to prevent young people, both native and immigrant, from leaving school. Instead they should aim to raise their level of education and opportunities on the labour market.

Immigration Will Not Balance an Aging Population in Germany

Spiegel

Der Spiegel is a German newspaper. In the following viewpoint, the author says that Germany faces falling population, which may significantly reduce its working-age population and make its social welfare policies unsustainable. The German government had hoped that family-friendly policies would increase the birthrate and that immigration would increase and help make up the rest of the gap. However, the author says, birthrates have not increased. Furthermore, immigration has slowed substantially and is therefore not likely to solve Germany's population problem.

As you read, consider the following questions:

1. According to the viewpoint, by how much will Germany's population fall in the next fifty years?

2. Are more people entering Germany or leaving Germany, and by how much, according to 2009 figures?

3. What are some reasons the viewpoint suggests that immigrants find Germany unattractive?

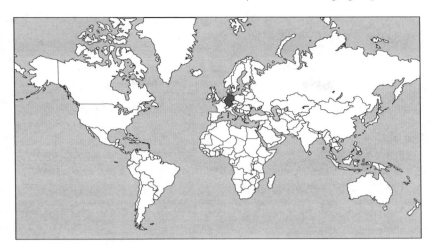

Germans fretting about the country's looming demographic problems are unlikely to have been cheered by recent news on birth rates and emigration. With its graying population, the country's cradle-to-grave welfare system could become unaffordable due to a dearth of working-age people to keep the system going. And the country seems to be failing to either attract enough immigrants or produce babies fast enough to dispel fears of future demographic disaster.

Hopes Dashed

Only two weeks ago [in May 2010], hopes of a government-created baby boom were dashed by the latest birth rate figures. The Federal Statistics Office revealed that despite heavy investment in maternity and paternity pay and other family-friendly policies, the birth rate was actually declining in Germany, with 651,000 children born in 2009, fully 30,000 less than in 2008.

With an average of just 1.38 children being born to each woman, the birth rate is not high enough to keep the population stable. The aging country will find it hard to secure the tax revenues to support all those pensioners of the future or to maintain economic growth. In fact, demographers expect

Germany's population to fall by 17 million from the current 82 million over the next 50 years.

Now adding to the woes are the latest migration figures which show that more people are actually leaving Germany than choosing to make the country their new home. For a quarter of a century, Germany had been a country of net immigration but in 2008 that trend was reversed. The figures for 2009, while showing a slight improvement, are still worrying. On Wednesday, the Federal Statistics Office released figures showing that 13,000 more people had left Germany in 2009 than had arrived.

In total 734,000 people opted to leave the country last year, while only 721,000 immigrated. Although the immigration total showed an increase of 39,000 over 2008, at the beginning of the decade over 800,000 people were choosing to make Germany their home each year.

With an average of just 1.38 children being born to each woman, the birth rate is not high enough to keep the population stable.

Most of those who chose to leave were foreigners returning home, with the prime destinations being Poland (123,000), Romania (44,000) and Turkey (40,000). Of the 155,000 Germans who chose to leave their homeland, most favored the US and Switzerland.

There was a slight dip in emigration, with 4,000 fewer people leaving than in 2008. The global recession is thought to have been a contributing factor here, as prospective emigrants know they will have a tougher time securing jobs abroad. Spain, for example, had long been a popular choice for German emigrants but its high unemployment figures are now acting as a deterrent.

"Not Exactly Inviting"

Klaus J. Bade, the chairman of the Expert [Council of German Foundations on] Integration and Migration (SVR), argues that Germany has to make itself more attractive to Germans and immigrants alike. He says that many people leaving Germany complain of the "narrow hierarchies in German companies, the poor chances of getting ahead and the lack of fairness in recognizing performance." On the other hand, people in other countries are put off by Germany's reputation for not welcoming foreigners, an image "that is not exactly inviting," Bade told the *Hamburger Abendblatt* newspaper.

Uta Koch of the Hamburg-based relief agency Raphaels Werk, which advises emigrants and returning migrants, says that opting to leave home has little to do with seeking adventure. "Most people find it difficult to leave Germany," she told the *Die Welt* newspaper. The decision is made out of a fear of unemployment at home, or the hope of better pay and child care abroad, she explains.

The Green Party migration expert Memet Kilic says that figures show that "our country is no longer so attractive, particularly to migrants." He points to the fact that there are now 10,000 more people leaving Germany for Turkey than coming the other way.

Germany has to make itself more attractive to Germans and immigrants alike.

Reiner Klingholz of the Berlin Institute for Population and Development meanwhile told the business daily *Handelsblatt* that for the economy to make up for the falling birth rates there would need to be "an additional half a million people immigrating per year until 2050—and that is not likely."

Periodical and Internet Sources Bibliography

The following articles have been selected to supplement the diverse views presented in this chapter.

John Bingham	"Immigration Slows Rate of Ageing Population, Official Figures Suggest," *Telegraph*, March 2, 2012.
Lena Calahorrano	"Population Aging and Individual Attitudes Toward Immigration: Disentangling Age, Cohort and Time Effects," IDEAS, 2011. http://ideas.repec.org/p/diw/diwsop/diw_sp389.html.
Economist	"Pensions: 70 or Bust!," April 7, 2011.
Michael Hodin	"Harness the Economic Power of an Aging Population," *Fiscal Times*, January 17, 2012.
Kyung Lah	"Plan Would Pay Japanese Families to Have Kids," CNN.com, September 4, 2009. http://edition.cnn.com/2009/WORLD/asiapcf/09/04/japan.children/index.html.
Christiane Nickel, Philipp Rother, and Angeliki Theophilopoulou	"Population Ageing and Public Pension Reforms in a Small Open Economy," IDEAS, February 2008. http://ideas.repec.org/p/ecb/ecbwps/20080863.html.
Adam Ozimek	"Does an Aging Population Hurt the Economy?," *Forbes*, February 7, 2013.
Mike Steketee	"Immigration No Cure-All for the Country's Ageing Population," *Australian*, October 3, 2009.
Xinhua News Agency	"OECD Calls for Further Pension Reforms to Cope with Aging Population," March 17, 2011. http://news.xinhuanet.com/english2010/world/2011-03/17/c_13784524.htm.

CHAPTER 3

Attitudes toward
the Elderly

The Elderly Enjoy High Status in Iran

Maryam Ala Amjadi

Maryam Ala Amjadi is an Iranian poet, translator, and essayist. In the following viewpoint, she argues that the elderly in Iran have traditionally been revered and respected. She says that reverence continues today. She explains that the elderly are seen as a source of wisdom and that they often are asked to resolve disputes. Many proverbs highlight the importance Iranians ascribe to the elderly. Ala Amjadi also points to the Kahrizak Charity Foundation, which cares for the indigent elderly free of charge.

As you read, consider the following questions:

1. What is Asis Vang, and what is its significance?
2. What is the Ladies Charitable Society of the Kahrizak Charity Foundation (KCF)?
3. What does Ala Amjadi say about the Iranian attitude toward nursing homes?

If you really want to hear heartfelt stories about the city and get a good taste of the true Iran, then you probably would have to sit in a taxi in Tehran [the capital of Iran] and strike a conversation with the driver. By the time you reach your des-

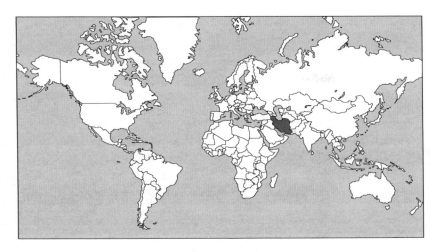

tination, you would not only have a firsthand political, social, financial and cultural analysis of the overall situation of the country but you may also find that in the process of the conversation you have opened up to a total stranger about what ails you most of all. It is as though you are taking a trip within a trip, riding the car and sharing a mental journey, perhaps on a therapeutic road. Besides, conversation makes the distance seem shorter. And Tehran's taxi drivers make shrewd critics of the past and the present, assuming the future as simply predictable with their wild interest in details.

"Hormat"

One of the most common stories that one hears is about difference between the past and the present generation, mostly a vivid glorification of the past and how "hormat" (literally meaning, reverence) particularly regarding the elders and the elderly were observed more than today, how the walls of "haya" (literally meaning, coyness and bashful politeness) and modesty have been run down by our hurried modern life.

Although this may be true to some extent, particularly in the capital and major cities, compared to other places, one can still witness a good deal of instances of respect and high regard for the elders. Marked by wrinkles of experience and white hair earned through the vicissitudes of life, elder family members are still considered as the "barkat" (literally meaning, blessings that generate prosperity) of the house, qualified individuals in the school of life whose words of wisdom one should cherish and live up to. In fact, there is a saying in the Persian language which the elderly often use, pertaining to the value of lessons learned by old age: "I have not whitened my hair in the mills." (Meaning: I have earned my experiences through hardships of life and know things. It is not easy to fool me.)

White hair and white beard have always been used as signifiers of reverence for old age wisdom and honoring the elders in the Iranian culture. In fact, even today if an elderly person and a young one fall into the pitfalls of disagreement, it is expected that the young would observe the "hormat" of the elder's white hair and white beard, probably keep silent and not retort.

White hair and white beard have always been used as signifiers of reverence for old age wisdom and honoring the elders in the Iranian culture.

Greeting the elders is, of course, a must in the Iranian culture and a sign of polite behavior. Standing up in respect before them and never stretching one's legs or raising one's voice in their presence are also deemed as good manners.

Despite their declining physical or mental health, the elderly are never truly casted out of social and family functions. In fact, they still continue to play a significant role in the lives of their immediate family members. In the mosque, the first rows of the communal prayers are where the elders of the community stand and pray while others line up behind them. Previously, if a wife had a row with her husband and left the house for her father's, it was always expected that an elder member of the family would intervene and make truce between the couple. The elders still seem to have a say in husband-wife conflicts, particularly in rural areas. Their presence and opinion in the traditional pre-marriage meeting of parents and the youth—known as "khastegaari" (literally meaning, demanding a bride)—is still of importance. After the wedding ceremony, it is also upon the elder members of the family to host the "paa goshaee" feast (literally meaning, opening the feet) whereby the newlyweds are received and welcomed home a few days after the official wedding.

The question is whether the youth-centered modern life and its constant emphasis on "individuality" could really and eventually wipe off our regard for our old accustomed traditions and good manners? One would think that "decorum" and "good manners" are never out of fashion.

Once on a long drive across the town, a taxi driver in Tehran shared the following anecdote with me.

"When I was a child, I used to come home from school and my mother would ask me to slow down, 'Shush! Your father is asleep. Be careful not to wake him up' and now when I come home from a long day's work, I hear my wife say 'Shush! The children are sleeping. Take care you don't wake them up.' I feel I am a victim of two generations!"

"Respecting mothers is better than going to Haj" [is one] *of the proverbs that show[s] the value of respect for parents and elders above anything and anyone.*

When Old Is Indeed Gold

Ancient Iran was among the first civilizations to appoint an annual day (16th of September) to honor the elderly and pay gratitude to the contribution of its seniors. Known as Asis Vang, this ceremonious day dates back to at least 3000 years according to some records. In fact, not only [were] senior citizens never fully isolated from the social scene but they also contributed their wisdom and experience towards betterment of the lifestyle of the others. For instance, naming a newborn was previously the task of the eldest in the family, known as "rish sefid" (literally meaning, white-beard). One could say that the custom is somehow still alive in small towns and villages. Seven days after birth, after a feast and gathering, the infant is placed in the arms of the eldest family member (usually a grandparent or great uncle) and he is asked to pick a name. The white-beard will then write a few names on a piece of paper and keep it between the pages of the Quran. He will then recite azan (call for prayer in Arabic) in the infant's right ear and a few other Islamic verses in his left ear. After this, he will pull out one of the paper slots and read aloud the name and all those present will approve by saying "salawat" ("Peace be upon him" is a phrase that Muslims often say after saying or hearing the name of the prophet of Islam). In some rural places, there is also a custom known as "roog-oshaei" (literally meaning, opening the face) which involves an elder (usually a grandmother or grandaunt) opening and unveiling the face of the newborn after his first bath. The elder pushes away the towel or any other wrapping from the baby's face and greets it with a smile. It is believed that if a good-natured, good-humored and happy person greets the baby, he will grow up to have a happy smiling face.

The white-beard was not only a part of other people's joy but he was also someone that people looked up to and counted on in times of trouble. If a neighbor or a member of a certain community was in financial trouble, the elders would make an effort to help them through a ritual known as "golrizoon" (literally meaning, casting flowers) which was a euphemism for donating money to an anonymous cause. Trusting their elders, people would willingly donate money to help out a person in need whose name was concealed out of fear of embarrassment. The custom is still alive in some parts of the country. Modern variations include charity boxes known as sandoghe-e-sadaghaat (box for alms) set up across all cities in Iran and the call for donations to social and cultural causes often broadcasted on the television, radio and billboards. Also, in times of conflict, particularly in case of divorce, arguments among siblings, parents and offspring, neighbors and other community members, elders were expected to intervene, help in resolving the issue and make peace. Their role was significant because it was axiomatic that persons involved in the conflict would hopefully listen to their elders, act upon their wishes and work out a way of compromise out of respect. In fact, white-beard slang has found its way into pop culture. "Let's resolve this white-beard style", is something you may hear from young people involved in an argument, which actually means, "Let's talk about this peacefully and work it out in a civilized manner".

Youth and the White-Beard Culture

No one can argue with the fact that elders are appreciated and revered to a great extent in Iran. Although modern youth culture, particularly in major cities, has naturally created a rift and conflict with the previous generation, respecting elders and the elderly still tops the social and cultural ladder of manners. In fact, Persian literature (didactic literature in particular) is replete with instances that emphasize the importance of regarding elders with eyes of respect and valuing their words of wisdom. Persian proverbs, too, offer a great deal of advice to the youth on their mannerism with the elderly. These proverbs can roughly be divided into two major groups: A- Proverbs that emphasize glorification of the elderly and acknowledgement of their wisdom and experience, hence the earned respect: "Have some respect for his white hair", "What the young man sees in the mirror, the old man sees in pure adobe" and "An old mind is worth more than the fortune of youth" are some prime examples. B- Proverbs that mainly depict the disadvantages of old age and pertinent physical conditions. These proverbs are actually the flip side of youth: "Old age is adorned with one thousand and one causes (illnesses)", "Buy lame, buy blind, just don't buy old" and "There is no pleasure in being an old king" are some examples that embolden the value of youth and youthful energy, as the past life of the elderly. Respecting elders, revering the elderly, parents and even those who apparently seem a bit older than us is considered a must and violation of this unsaid agreement could cause social and cultural downfall in the eyes of the public. "War with one's father is humiliation and bad omen", "Children can be found, but parents never" and "Respecting mothers is better than going to Haj [the Muslim pilgrimage to Mecca]" are some of the proverbs that show the value of respect for parents and elders above anything and anyone. Even Islamic sayings and teachings which are deeply intertwined with Iranian culture, regard respect for parents and elders as the first commandment after worshipping God. The prophet of Islam, Mohammad (PBUH [peace be upon him]), says, "Blessings lie with your elders." And "He who is not kind to children and respectful of elders and the elderly is not one of us". To have the blessings of one's elders (parents and grandparents in particular) is believed to bring blessings and good omen to one's life. Many people believe in gaining the approval of their parents, particularly mothers as an auspicious act.

Also greeting one another and saying hello is greatly stressed in Islamic teachings, but it is mostly customary for the youth to greet the elders as a sign of respect. Usually when an elder enters a room or a gathering, it is upon the young to stand up and greet them. Their words and experiences are redeemed as pearls of wisdom. In fact, if a family conflict (such as divorce, arguments between siblings) emerges, it is expected that the white beard of the family (or the elders who are of age) can help in resolving the issue as hopefully the youth would not disregard the words and advice of their elders.

House for the Elderly, Home to the Disabled

Founded in 1971 by the late Dr. Mohammad Reza Hakimzadeh in a small, derelict and underequipped house in southern Tehran, today the Kahrizak Charity Foundation (KCF), has thrived into a well-furnished, pristine, modern and spacious establishment where the elderly and disabled with no financial support are cared for, free of charge. What was initially a one-bed, one-patient room has now expanded into a 1600-bed center. The KCF, a private, nongovernmental, nonprofit, charitable organization, is situated in Kahrizak, in Rey County of Tehran Province. Known as the center for living, education and rehabilitation predominantly for the elderly, the KCF officially defines itself as a "place for living and not merely staying alive", a beautiful motto to which it has strived to live up to. And its mission: To deliver "personalized and professional care" and restore the "dignity of individuals" and improve the quality of their lives as much as possible. As a matter of fact, one could say that the KCF has blossomed into a well-constructed and coordinated city within a city. The establishment is surrounded by gardens, lawns and pools which enhance the beauty of the space. An integral part of the KCF is also the Ladies Charitable Society (LCS) founded by a group of dedicated, philanthropic women who decided to coordinate their humanitarian efforts in pursuit of assistance those they offered to the KCF. In 1998, the LCS was recognized as [an] NGO [nongovernmental organization] with special consultative status by the Economic and Social Council of the United Nations (ECOSOC). Also the Mother and Child Center, affiliated with the LCS was founded in 1990 to aid children who became orphaned after the devastating earthquake in Roodbar, Gilan [Province].

Facts About the Elderly

1. Although 60 plus individuals are almost universally known as seniors, the national health committee for seniors in Iran has declared 70 years as the age for senior citizens.

2. As of 2011, the overall life expectancy for Iranian citizens is 71.14 years, with a male life expectancy of 69.65 years and a female life expectancy of 72.72 years.

3. Iran has a population of over 5 million elderly citizens which makes about 7.3 percent of the country's total population. 51.8 percent of the senior population are males and 48.2 percent are females. Interestingly more than 88 percent of senior males and 51 percent of senior females are married.

4. It is predicted that Iran will have an estimated senior population of 26,393,000 individuals by 2050 which would make about 26 percent of the total population.

5. As of 2011, more than 16,853 individuals aged 100 years or more are living in Iran.

6. Gilan Province in north Iran ranks first in the country's senior population.

7. In Iran, elderly relatives are usually kept at home, not placed in a nursing home. It is still a kind of social stigma to put one's parents in a nursing home if an immediate family member is alive.

8. Although there are professional geriatricians in Iran, one could say that geriatrics is a relatively new field of medicine and practice in the country as senior citizens are in the habit of referring to general practitioners.

9. There is also a growing trend of marriage among senior citizens. Previously eyed as a not-so-acceptable act by the public, more and more people are becoming open to marriage among seniors.

Born in 1893, Mohammad Tayeb Khalili Shahmirzadi is Iran's and the world's oldest man alive. The 118-year-old who was in good health and shape until some time ago is presently admitted to a hospital due to physical ailments pertinent to old age. Prior to this, all his acquaintances never recall him taking any medicine or going anywhere by car. Speaking to reporters, his 40-year-old granddaughter said that her grandfather always ate simple food in less quantity and if he fell ill, he would fast for 3 days in order to clear and cleanse his body from the disease. Although his house was distanced from his workplace, he would always make an effort to go by walking and every week he would travel on foot to the Shah Abdol Azim Shrine or the Friday Prayer venue. Shahmirzadi who has been schooled up to the 8th grade (junior high school) has taught reading and writing to many of his friends. His granddaughter believes his dedication to prayer and reading books as the secret to his long life.

Denmark Has Excellent Services for the Elderly

Judy Steed

Judy Steed is a columnist at the Toronto Star. *In the following viewpoint, she reports on elder care in Denmark. She says that the Danes work hard to keep the elderly in their own homes by providing as many services as needed. In cases where long-term care in an institution is needed, the goal remains to reduce dependency as much as possible and to make sure the elderly have full and fulfilling lives. Steed concludes that elder care in Denmark is more expensive than in Canada but that it is much more humane.*

As you read, consider the following questions:

1. When and how does regular monitoring of an elderly person's needs begin in Denmark, and why is this important?
2. How many people do Danish home-service workers visit, and what is their salary?
3. Why does Steed not look forward to her visit to the home for people suffering from dementia?

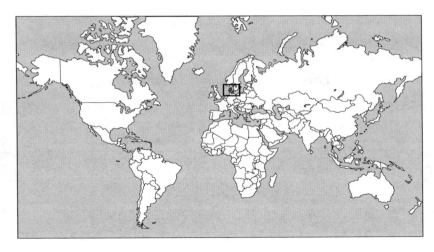

I t's a balmy afternoon in Tivoli Gardens, the legendary amusement park in the Danish capital. Lots of older women are out walking in the sunshine, which surprises me and my travel companion, Toronto gerontologist Margaret Mac-Adam—we don't normally see so many elderly people leaning on walkers and canes, looking vital and happy, in Toronto parks.

Old, but Staying at Home

Else, 91, beautiful in a yellow sweater and colourful scarf, re-laxes on a bench with her granddaughter Karin, who trans-lates for Else.

The two meet here once a month, Else coming by train, Karin by bike. "I used to bike a lot," Else says, "but I stopped when I turned 90. . . . Still, I like to spend the day at Tivoli Gardens with my granddaughter."

A widow—her husband died 20 years ago—Else has lived alone in the same apartment for many years. She's had hip re-placement surgery and is considering knee replacement.

She recalls that when she turned 75, she had the standard outreach visit from a local nurse, who assessed her needs, offered any modifications to her apartment that were necessary, and promised to keep an eye on her, to see when she might need help at home.

Else now has a cleaner once a week and someone to help with grocery shopping. "That's all," she says, straightening her back. "I do my own cooking. I can look after myself."

Will she move to a nursing home one day? "No. I like to close the door and have my privacy."

"I used to bike a lot," Else says, "but I stopped when I turned 90."

In terms of services that elderly people actually want, Denmark—and neighbouring Sweden—are the best places in the world to grow old. Both have strong cradle-to-grave social programs, and compete with each other—and with their Scandinavian cousins Norway and Finland—to give their citizens the best comprehensive elder care.

Danish and Swedish policies are designed to help people stay at home as long as possible through a variety of home-care services and regular house calls by doctors. In Denmark, regular monitoring of an elderly person's needs begins with a visit by a nurse when a person turns 75. "That visit has a huge impact," MacAdam observes. "It reassures and also educates the individual."

I am struck by the attitude of proud independence I encounter in many of the seniors I meet in the two countries, how they persist in doing the chores they are able to do. The system supports them where needed, but doesn't take over—not even in nursing homes, where they have kitchenettes so they can make their own toast and tea. "The philosophy is that, no matter how frail, you have a right to be in charge of your life," MacAdam says.

More Money, Better Philosophy

In the past 20 years, Denmark focused so much on home care that it stopped building long-term care facilities. Now Danes are finding they need a few, and they're leading the world in creating small (by Ontario standards) nursing homes where the focus is on what people can do.

Many long-term care facilities in Denmark and Sweden are homey, intimate environments where quality of life is paramount. Fresh flowers on dining room tables, wine with meals and real camaraderie among staff and residents are among the hallmarks.

Such facilities contrast starkly with most in North America, where residents often have nothing to do. Despite the best efforts of recreational staff to organize cookie-baking or art classes, the overall paradigm of elder dependency prevails.

"The philosophy is that no matter how frail, you have a right to be in charge of your life."

The quality of long-term care in Denmark and Sweden reflects their relatively generous spending on the sector. According to Organisation for Economic Co-operation and Development figures, in 2005 Denmark devoted 2.6 per cent of its gross domestic product [GDP] to long-term care, and Sweden 3.3 per cent. By contrast, Canada spent 1.2 per cent of its GDP, and the U.S., .9 per cent.

But Danish and Swedish success is about more than money; it's about philosophy.

As MacAdam and I toured Danish facilities earlier this year [2008], and then I went off to Sweden on my own, I was impressed by the engagement of most older Scandinavians, their sense of belonging. In contrast, North American elders often feel sidelined. The ageism that is so much a part of North American society didn't hit me until I saw the vitality of older people in Denmark and Sweden.

We drop in at Frederiksberg Home Service, a public agency in Copenhagen. Simone Eliasson, a senior manager, explains that her office is responsible for the home care of 3,000 clients.

Almost one-quarter of older Danes get some level of home care, and they can choose the provider from public or private agencies. The amount of service they get is determined by the municipality's home-care manager, who assesses whether they need help with personal care, house cleaning or food preparation.

Tine Rostgaard, a senior researcher at the Danish National Centre for Social Research and an expert in care of the aged, emphasizes that "the philosophy of the Danish government is to integrate elderly people, to keep them active in the community as long as possible, to not do things for them when they can do for themselves."

If a man loses his wife, who has done all the cooking, "we will teach him to cook, instead of providing food. You should continue to learn and develop through your life span."

The ageism that is so much a part of North American society didn't hit me until I saw the vitality of older people in Denmark and Sweden.

Reducing Dependency

Dependency, the Danes have learned, is a slippery slope that hastens your demise. But "when you're old and frail," adds Rostgaard, "the care should come to you." Hence the routine practice of home visits by health professionals such as doctors.

The government has studied the cost-effectiveness of the preventive home visits to every 75-year-old, "and our outcome studies show they are highly effective," Rostgaard says.

Certainly, the age-75 visit means the Danes avoid a problem we face in Ontario: Most people don't know what home care is available or how to access it.

Danish home-service workers visit up to seven people a day. They make about $30 an hour (in Ontario, comparable home-care employees earn about $15). It can be a tough job, says Thea Andersen, 30. After 12 years of providing personal care for elders, she's burned out.

"The government is making cutbacks," she says, "and clients can't be guaranteed to get the same worker all the time, which makes it hard for elders, having to cope with strangers coming to their home."

The Danish government has applied tighter cost controls on home service: The hours of care available to clients have been cut, with cleaning reduced from weekly to once every two weeks. "It used to be more relaxed," Andersen says. "If the elder was sad and wanted you to stay longer and talk, you could do it. Now it's more rigid. The worker has to watch the clock and get to the next person."

Perhaps it's the pressure on home-care workers, and the lack of social status, respect and support, that contribute to a labour shortage in this sector not only in Scandinavia but throughout the developed world. The trends are similar in Denmark and Canada: Personal-support work is often seen as an entry-level job; immigrants often take these jobs, but they may have difficulty with language skills and writing reports; elderly clients may feel uncomfortable with workers who aren't familiar with the language or culture. When dementia is part of the scenario, employees can be subjected to abuse.

Dementia, but Not Depression

MacAdam and I take the train to a pleasant Copenhagen residential suburb to visit Torndalshave, a group home for people with dementia. I am not looking forward to this visit. My father, who suffered from Alzheimer's [disease], was "incarcerated"—his word—in a long-term care facility in Ottawa for

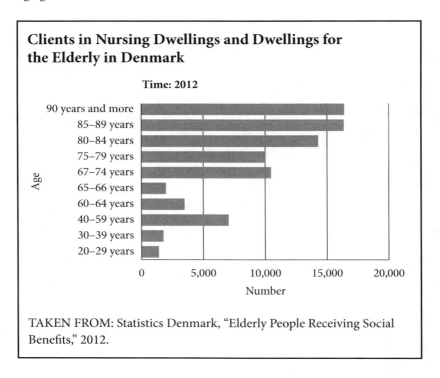

Clients in Nursing Dwellings and Dwellings for the Elderly in Denmark

Time: 2012

TAKEN FROM: Statistics Denmark, "Elderly People Receiving Social Benefits," 2012.

five years before his death. My old friend Joyce Wieland, the artist, suffered from early-onset Alzheimer's and spent the last few years of her life bent over in a dementia ward.

Dementia is not a pretty thing, and the places I've seen in Ontario, though clean and well run, are profoundly depressing. With Celeste, my therapy dog—she's certified to visit nursing homes, and she started me on this journey into aging when she got her first job—I've visited dementia wards; mostly the residents sit in their rooms, with a TV blaring in the corner. Or they pace. Or stare into space.

Here at Torndalshave, the mood is light and bright. Partly it's the architecture. The one-story building is new and modern, with a courtyard garden in the centre. The inner walls are glass, floor to ceiling. Light pours in. Flowers and tomato plants thrive in the garden, where residents help out.

There are only 12 residents, which amazes MacAdam. "We would never build a dementia home in Ontario for only 12 people," she tells me. "It's great for the residents, but we would say it's not cost-effective."

The residents live in two pods of six, with two staff members caring for each pod. They have their own living room with an attached, open-concept kitchen; residents can enjoy the bustle and aromas of food being prepared, and they can help make the meals. If you can peel potatoes, you are enlisted.

Staff, along with residents, do all the cooking from scratch, plus laundry and cleaning. It's deliberate policy: to engage the people who live here to participate in household chores. If you can hold a broom, you sweep the floor. And residents can have a glass of wine at dinner. (In Ontario nursing homes, you can buy a bottle of wine, but you can't drink it in the dining room; a glass will be brought to your room if you ask.)

As in Ontario, residents pay their rent from their old-age pension. If they need a subsidy from the municipality, they get it. But unlike Ontario, where dementia wards are locked, it's against the law in Denmark and Sweden to lock people in.

The biggest surprise for me is the behaviour of the residents: They don't seem depressed. They sit in the living room, a few at a table, interacting with staff. A small terrier named Ouzo sniffs around. "Ouzo," says a man, "come here." Ouzo jumps up on his lap.

A Model System

An old woman holds and rocks a doll back and forth, as if it's a baby. A few men smoke. One fellow kisses MacAdam's hand. We observe the genuine warmth between workers and residents.

Hanne Hannssan, a manager who greets residents with hugs, says she's old enough to retire. "I have a pension and I don't need to be here, but I love the work." Love the work? With dementia patients?

Residents' rooms are private and spacious, decorated with the individuals' own furniture, and include a sink, a two-burner hot plate, a small fridge and cupboards—so family members can make a cup of coffee, have a bite to eat.

The biggest surprise for me is the behaviour of the residents: They don't seem depressed.

MacAdam is wowed. "This is a model project. It's the Rose Kennedy School of long-term care. Rose Kennedy lived in her own home with three registered practical nurses and her family came to visit. This is as close to that as you'll ever get in a public system."

We go on to Lotte, the most famous nursing home in Denmark. We walk up the path through a beautiful garden to a large old Copenhagen villa. An off-kilter fellow of 93, one of 23 residents, steps off the elevator. He is wearing a helmet to protect his head—he has a tendency to fall—and pushing a walker. The helmet is indicative of the lively life Lotte residents lead; instead of not going out, you wear a helmet and take the risk.

The villa's big windows are open for the early summer breezes. Fresh flowers dance on all the tables in the dining room. Fancy chandeliers hang from the ceiling.

In another room, a few men watch soccer on a giant, flat-screen TV. Jan, seated on the sofa, is smoking. He takes a small pack out of his shirt pocket. "They give me 10 cigarettes in the morning, 10 more in the afternoon."

I ask what's good about the place.

I receive the answer I will hear repeatedly throughout Denmark and Sweden. "The best thing about this place is the people. This is home."

He moved to Lotte after suffering a brain aneurysm and a stroke. "I was lucky to get in here. The food is good. I like to go outside and walk in the neighbourhood. I play cards."

"What's special about this place is that it really is home-like," MacAdam observes. "It's not at all like an institution, and it would never be legal in Ontario. It would not meet fire safety codes; there are no fire doors. Look at all the smokers. This kind of place has been outlawed in North America."

Maybe we've regulated our nursing homes to death?

"It's true that you can overregulate facilities," MacAdam allows.

The Danish government, acknowledging that it needs more up-to-date nursing homes, is modernizing old facilities and building new ones like Torndalshave.

The biggest, a 150-person building, is currently being reno-vated and downsized to hold 100. The current Danish ideal— the result of an international architectural competition—is the Flintholm Care Home, an oval-shaped building in Frederiks-berg with 56 units, 13 rooms to a floor, surrounding a com-munal dining and living area, which means every suite has ex-terior windows and there are no long corridors. No long corridors is a priority. Every unit has its own bathroom and kitchenette.

Better Efficiencies, Lower Quality Office

The total cost of a Danish nursing-home room is about $75,000 per year, the same as in Sweden. "Very expensive," says MacAdam. "In Ontario, the total cost per person is $43,000 a year. We get better financial efficiencies from our larger build-ings." And poorer quality of life.

A few days later, we return to Lotte to meet with its fa-mous director, Thyra Frank. Dinner has been delivered: open-faced sandwiches with smoked salmon and shrimp. The staff bring out bottles of wine—good wine—and schnapps. "We cook during the week, but on weekends," says a staff member, "we order in. I love working with older people," the staffer adds. "They are so appreciative of what you do for them."

"Do you have enough staff?" MacAdam asks.

She's startled when the reply is, "Yes, we do. We have four to five staff during the day for 24 people."

"In Ontario, if you ask that question," MacAdam tells me, "you're always told no, no, we don't have enough staff."

As dinnertime approaches, residents make their way to the dining room. The piano player arrives, a spiffy showman with blow-dried hair. He plays songs the residents are familiar with. They tap their fingers and canes in time to the music.

A group of Norwegian social workers has descended on Lotte; they tell us they want nursing homes in Norway to become more like this.

> "In Ontario if you ask that question . . . you're always told no, no, we don't have enough staff."

Family Members Always Welcome

Thyra Frank enters the dining room. A large, affectionate woman who hugs everyone in her path, she invites us to her table, pours us wine, insists we eat, and talks about what she believes: that all of us deserve a warm home and a sense of belonging till the day we die. Family members are always welcome to join residents for lunch or dinner, at no charge. "Of course," says Frank, "this is their home—of course their families must be comfortable and welcome."

She talks about the annual holidays for Lotte residents and staff, to Spain or Greece, involving everyone, including people suffering from dementia. The holidays are paid for out of the sick-pay fund, which Lotte is able to keep since no one calls in sick.

The adult daughter of a woman with dementia says she was surprised when her mother was taken on a trip to Spain. "I thought people with dementia were so confused, there was no point," she says. But when her mother returned, "she was happy. I could see that she'd had a good time."

All of us deserve a warm home and a sense of belonging till the day we die.

The party went on late into the night, with after-dinner liqueurs served to everyone, including the residents, who stayed until the end.

Should sleep not come, they will not receive a sleeping pill. Lotte has a better idea—a glass of schnapps, or three.

The Elderly Face Age Discrimination in Australia

Kate Southam

Kate Southam is a workplace writer and coach, as well as the founding editor of CareerOne.com.au; she blogs at Cube Farmer. *In the following viewpoint, she discusses an Australian human rights report that found systematic age discrimination in Australia. The report says that workers over forty-five are seen as less capable, less able to adjust to change, and as generally less desirable than younger workers. Southam says that age discrimination is one of the last acceptable forms of prejudice, and she urges Australians to work to fight it.*

As you read, consider the following questions:

1. How are "mature age workers" officially defined, according to Southam?
2. What issues besides employment are flagged as examples of ageism in the report Southam discusses?
3. What places does Southam suggest have less discrimination against the elderly than does Australia?

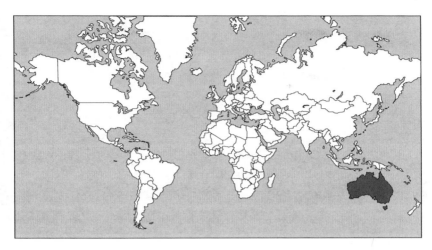

When did Australia get so ageist about oldies?

The commissioner responsible for age discrimination, Elizabeth Broderick, thinks it's a good question and says the answer is something the nation should grapple with together.

Prejudice and Misinformation

Today Broderick launches a new report by the Australian Human Rights Commission, "Age Discrimination—Exposing the Hidden Barrier for Mature Age Workers." Compiled from a range of research, academic papers and government studies, the report paints a picture of exclusion, ill-informed assumptions and even humiliation for older people in Australia.

Broderick, who is also the sex discrimination commissioner, hopes the report will "elevate" the conversation about prejudice that exists towards older workers in particular. She argues that given Australia's ageing workforce, ageism is as much an economic issue as a social justice issue.

By the way, "mature age workers" are officially defined as 45 or older.

According to the report, ageism is the systematic stereo-typing of, and discrimination against, people simply because they are older. Older people are not seen as individuals but rather lumped together.

For example, all older people are seen as a higher occupa-tional health & safety risk or unable to learn new technolo-gies.

The report suggests that ageism has worsened with the shift away from valuing experience to the "efficiency and com-pliance over quality model also known as the work intensifica-tion model. It is based on the thinking that older people are experienced but high risk and inefficient and younger people [are] inexperienced and compliant."

It looks at issues such as the way older people are screened out of the recruitment process by employers instructing a re-cruitment agency not to put forward any candidate for inter-view aged over 40, or job interviews conducted by young people unable to identify with older candidates.

While employers cannot specify age in a job ad, the report claims words such as "innovative", "dynamic" and "creative" are code for "young".

All older people are seen as a higher occupational health & safety risk or unable to learn new technologies.

Once at work older employees are passed over for promo-tion or denied training because they are not deemed worth the investment of time and money. When it comes to redun-dancies older people are often targeted as "dead wood" and the first to go.

Issues Beyond Employment

The report focuses on employment but it does flag several other issues associated with age prejudice towards older people.

Age Discrimination in Australia

A lot of age discrimination comes from negative stereotypes of ageing. Our society tolerates a range of negative stereotypes about older people, for example all older people are mentally and physically weak, stubborn, out of date, unable to learn, seriously unhealthy, in all, a burden to society. When a society accepts these images, it is not surprising that older people are treated worse just because of their age, in employment, in financial and other important services, in having their views and choices respected. In other words they are subjected to age discrimination. Not only are they denied fair treatment, but this negative stereotyping actually damages their health. . . .

One study of 660 individuals . . . found that people who expressed a positive self-perception of ageing tended to have a survival advantage of 7.5 years over those who expressed negative self-perception of ageing.

Susan Ryan,
"The Rights of Older People and Age Discrimination in Australia,"
Australian Human Rights Commission, November 22, 2012.

The lucrative anti-aging industry offering everything from drugs to cosmetic surgery reinforces "the belief that old age is repugnant . . . promising relief to those who can pay." And on television screens older people are too often portrayed as "bumbling, crotchety or senile".

In the health sector, symptoms in older patients such as balance problems, memory loss and depression are dismissed from the outset as 'old age' instead of treatable conditions.

Broderick says age discrimination is "entrenched" in Australia and can be found in almost every sphere of public life.

She believes we need a social movement not unlike [the] women's movement to free us from our mind-set that aging is something to fear and fight.

"We need social change within the community. [Ageism] doesn't just exist—it thrives," says Broderick adding that unlike other forms of discrimination ageism is not yet "at the point of being stigmatised."

In other words, it's socially acceptable to be ageist towards older people.

Over the years I have received hundreds of emails from mature age workers detailing their war with prejudice at work. One man in his 50s told me of being shocked by the level of ageism here when he returned home from years in America. He eventually left our shores and found a good job in Hong Kong. When I published his comments I was inundated with emails from Australians in their 50s and 60s who had returned to Europe, North America or Asia so they could resume their careers.

[Commissioner Elizabeth Broderick] believes we need a social movement not unlike [the] women's movement to free us from our mind-set that aging is something to fear and fight.

For the older people reading this, I would love to hear your views on whether you feel you have been discriminated against due to age. To be fair, I'd also like to know if you held clichéd views about older people when you were young.

And young people, be honest and tell me how you want to be treated when you are 45 plus.

If this just becomes a young versus oldies beat-up session then we will miss an opportunity to think about whether Australia has created a society that excludes older people from work opportunities, wellness strategies and a dignified role in daily life.

While there is a lot of prejudice out there—and none of it good—ageism against older people is the issue that should get everyone's attention because if you are lucky and take good care of yourself it could happen to you one day.

Many Chinese Will Not Help the Elderly for Fear of Lawsuits

Feng Yiran

Feng Yiran is a journalist for the Epoch Times. *In the following viewpoint, he reports that many elderly Chinese fall, are unable to get up, and die. He says that passersby often are afraid to help old people who fall because of well-publicized incidents in which helpers were sued. Yiran says that new guidelines from the government do not address the fear of lawsuits and do little to address the problem.*

As you read, consider the following questions:

1. What happened to Mr. Li when he fell in front of a market in Wuhan, according to the viewpoint?
2. To what did *Southern Metropolis Daily* attribute Chinese people's reluctance to help the elderly?
3. What did Sina Weibo's poll find about Chinese people's willingness to help the elderly?

Recent guidelines by Chinese authorities on how to assist an elderly person who has fallen in the street have unleashed a debate among Chinese netizens. They are in a

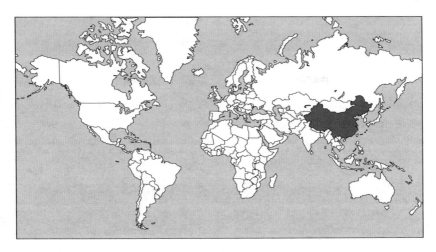

catch-22 between wanting to help, and a fear of being sued by predatory elderly fall victims. The government guidelines have piled insult upon injury, according to some netizens.

Falling Down

Falling down is a leading cause of death for Chinese citizens aged 65 and above, according to Yang Maowei, associate professor of the First Hospital of China Medical University. However, in recent years, there have been frequent reports of such deaths in public places with no one helping the victims, Yang said.

Falling down is a leading cause of death for Chinese citizens aged 65 and above.

It seems that Chinese people have become reluctant to help because they worry that the person they help may later turn around and sue them, as that is what's been happening a number of times in recent years. As a consequence, several elderly have been left to die in the streets with people passing by or watching, but not helping them.

On Dec. 29, 2010, an 83-year-old retired veteran, Mr. Zheng, fell while walking on a sidewalk in Fuzhou City of southeast China's Fujian Province. A handful of people stopped and looked on, but no one helped him. When the ambulance arrived, the man had already stopped breathing, *Southeast Express* reported.

Another similar case happened on Dec. 14, 2010, in a community of Shenzhen City when 78-year-old Mr. Xiao Yusheng fell and was left lying on the ground until his son found him 20 minutes later. None of the passersby tried to help, according to a report by *Southern Metropolis Daily*.

Most recently, an 88-year-old man, Mr. Li, fell on Sept. 2 [2011] in front of a market in Wuhan, less than 100 meters from his home. He tried to get up, but didn't have the strength, *Chutian Metropolis Daily* reported on Sept. 4.

A nearby vendor said that Mr. Li lay on the ground for one hour, with many people stopping to look at him, but no one helped him up. Eventually someone informed his family, and he was taken to a hospital, but he had already died of asphyxiation.

Mr. Li's 87-year-old wife, Zhou Juzhen, issued a statement three days later saying, "If I fall on the sidewalk, people who help me will not be held liable for any consequences."

Ms. Zhou said she wanted to remove people's fear of negative consequences in case she ever needed help in an emergency situation.

Fear of Helping

Southern Metropolis Daily said in a Sept. 9 report, "The Fear of Helping the Elderly Is the Real Sorrow," that the phenomenon reflects Chinese people's mistrust of society. The report cited three cases of people being sued after helping an elderly.

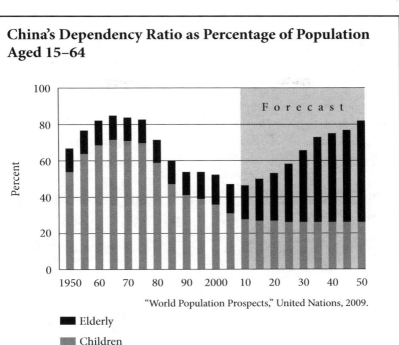

China's Dependency Ratio as Percentage of Population Aged 15–64

"World Population Prospects," United Nations, 2009.

■ Elderly
▨ Children

TAKEN FROM: China-Mike.com, "China's Population: A Looming Demographic Time Bomb," January 24, 2011.

In 2006, Peng Yu, in Nanjing, Jiangsu Province, helped an old lady who had fallen and broken a bone. She subsequently sued Peng, and the case went through three trials before the parties reached an agreement and the woman withdrew the case.

In another case in Tianjin in 2009, a Mrs. Wang fell down and was hurt when she illegally climbed over a roadside railing. Mr. Xu Yunhe, who happened to drive by, noticed her fall and stopped his car to help the old woman, bandaging her up and calling first aid.

Mrs. Wang, however, claimed that Xu's car had bumped into her and sued Xu in court. The court ruled that Xu should pay 100,000 yuan (US$15,654) in compensation.

On Aug. 26 of this year, Hong Bin, a bus driver, helped an old woman who had fallen in the street, but was accused of being the perpetrator. He was eventually exonerated through a monitoring video recording.

In 2006, Peng Yu, in Nanjing . . . helped an old lady who had fallen and broken a bone. She subsequently sued Peng.

These three cases have attracted nationwide attention, and are said to be the reason for Chinese people's reluctance of helping the elderly in emergency situations.

Ministry of Health Guidelines

Now China's Ministry of Health issued guidelines on Sept. 6 on how to handle cases of elderly falling. But instead of addressing the worrisome legal liability issue, it focuses mainly on medical consequences of a fall and offers technical solutions to different fall scenarios, while also telling people to overcome embarrassment and psychological fear of helping.

This has further inflamed citizens who feel in a catch-22 between wanting to help and having fear of being taken advantage of for their kindness.

One line in the guidelines that particularly irked netizens said, "whether or not to lend a hand depends on the situation."

After the ministry's guidelines came out, Sina Weibo conducted a poll, asking people whether they are still willing to help an elderly who has fallen, considering the ministry's guidelines.

Of the 5,031 who voted, only 20 percent said yes, while 43 percent said no, and the remaining 38 percent said they're not sure.

Some people left comments expressing their inner conflicts and disillusionment over China's sliding moral values:

"I dare not help, but I'll run to a public phone booth to call 120 [the emergency number in China], and ask for an ambulance."

"I can't even protect my own safety. How can I have the ability to take care of others? It's really funny!"

"To put it frankly, it reflects the degeneration of society's morality. The culture has no direction, the morality has no bottom line, and the trust between people, and between people and the government is too low."

Three cases have attracted nationwide attention, and are said to be the reason for Chinese people's reluctance of helping the elderly in emergency situations.

"Unless I were Bill Gates, I would help for sure."

"I would certainly help before. Now I'm really a bit afraid."

"In today's Chinese society, traditional values and virtues have been eradicated completely. No matter what guidelines are issued, when one really stands at a critical point, the law will not protect the poor people."

"There's no way out. The state educates us this way, and now it turns around to accuse us of having no morality. Isn't that ridiculous? Whether to help is not a moral issue, but the crux of China's current education."

"At present, China's social values are lost, and morality is ruined to the point of national doom."

India's Elderly Have Little Social Protection

K.S. Harikrishnan

K.S. Harikrishnan is a journalist for Inter Press Service. In the following viewpoint, he reports that India has no comprehensive policy to address the needs of elderly people. As a result, the elderly often have no choice but to be financially dependent on their families or to continue to work as long as they can. He contends that the country has a shortage of elder care homes and has serious problems caring for the elderly when they become ill. Harikrishnan concludes that India needs to establish more care and better policies for dealing with the old.

As you read, consider the following questions:

1. What does Dr. S. Irudaya Rajan say helped support elderly people in the past, and why has that support eroded?

2. To what does the "unorganized sector" of the economy refer?

3. What does Harikrishnan say the 2011 census data reveal about elderly Indians' living situations?

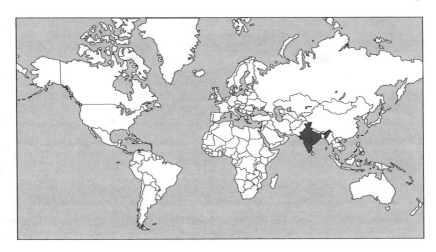

At midnight on Oct. 12 [2012], 91-year-old George Puthen-veettil, a widower living in Kalanjur village in the Patha-namthitta district of the southern Indian state of Kerala, was brutally tortured and ousted from his own house by his only son for "not earning any money".

Elder Insecurity

The nonagenarian wandered the streets of his village for hours before he reached a shelter in Pathanapuram with the help of neighbours. Police said the son had often beaten and harassed the old man, who was financially dependent on his son.

For many people like George, the sunset years of life turn out to be a traumatic period, in which they find themselves entirely dependent on families or friends due to the absence of a good social security system or government pension plan in India.

Expressing concern over the increasing insecurity of elders in the country, Dr. [S.] Irudaya Rajan, a prominent demographer and chair professor of the research unit on international migration under the Ministry of Indian Overseas Affairs, told IPS [Inter Press Service] that income security is one of the most urgent needs of India's aging population.

Years ago, "traditional values and religious beliefs were quite supportive of elderly people", he said.

Today, economic hardships and the faltering nuclear family system are "drastically eroding the support base of aged people".

"The majority of the elderly tend to work even after the age of retirement due to inadequate social security and financial resources," Rajan added.

A report on the aging population in India, released by the United Nations Population Fund (UNFP) in New Delhi, said that the country had 90 million elderly people in 2011, with the number expected to grow to 173 million by 2026.

Of the 90 million seniors, 30 million are living alone, and 90 percent work for a living.

Experts estimate that only eight percent of the labour force of about 460 million receives social security from an employer.

For many people ..., the sunset years of life turn out to be a traumatic period, in which they find themselves entirely dependent on families or friends.

"Informal" Labourers Left Out in the Cold

Over 94 percent of India's working population is part of the unorganised sector, which refers to all unlicensed, self-employed or unregistered economic activity such as owner-manned general stores, handicrafts and handloom workers, rural traders and farmers, among many others.

Gopal Krishnan, an economist in Chennai, told IPS "There is no social safety coverage for people in the unorganised sector, which accounts for half of the GDP (gross domestic product) of India".

According to the World Bank, India's GDP in 2011 was 1,848 billion dollars.

The Pension System in India

In traditional Indian society, family relationships and ethical values maintained an informal way of caring for the elderly. The complexity of modern society and a paradigm shift in the demographic scenario have resulted in an inadequacy of the informal elder-caring system. Available evidence suggests that the origin of social security in India dates back to the 3rd century BC. Different social assistance institutions and welfare centres used to be established during the ancient days in India, which were concerned with the relief and alleviation of sickness, poverty and distress.

In modern India, no universal social security system exists for the protection of the elderly against economic deprivation. Perhaps, higher levels of poverty and unemployment act as deterrents to the institution of a state pension scheme financed by a pay-roll tax for all the elderly. Instead, India has adopted social insurance and the pension policy that largely hinges on financing through the employer and employee participation and restricts the coverage to the organized sector workers. In this country, the most important state-sponsored (and also the unfunded pay-as-you-go (PAYG)) pension system covers only civil servants.

S. Irudaya Rajan and Syam Prasad,
"Pensions and Social Security in India," in Institutional Provisions
and Care for the Aged. *Eds. S. Irudaya Rajan, Carla Risseeuw,*
and Myrtle Perera. New York: Anthem Press, 2011, p. 118.

In 2006, the National Commission for Enterprises in the Unorganized Sector recommended that the Union Government establish a national social security scheme to provide the minimum level of benefits to workers retiring from the informal sector.

Until now, the government has not been able to compile a comprehensive policy to address the issues of elderly people. The ministry of social justice and empowerment drafted a national policy on older persons in 1999, which was never implemented.

Hardships Abound

Analysts point out that India's aging population is constantly grappling with health issues, economic stress, family matters, uncertain living arrangements, gender disparities, urban-rural differences, displacement and slum-like living conditions.

Dr. Udaya Shankar Mishra, a senior demographer at the Centre for Development Studies in Thiruvananthapuram, believes the current "profile" of the aging population of India can change.

"The (perception) of the elderly as a burden can, with suitable policies, be turned into an opportunity to realise active and healthy aging," he told IPS.

"With limited resources, we need to adopt viable policy changes to manage the crisis of the aged. This calls for a detailed auditing of (all) the affairs of the elderly, primarily health, morbidity and mortality in addition to economic and emotional well-being.

"Research on geriatric health needs to (shift) towards ensuring a better quality of life among future elderly persons. Considering the demographic inversion and its associated challenges, it (is clear) that investments into healthy aging are necessary," he added.

Data from the 2011 national census revealed that the percentage of aged living alone or with spouse is as high as 45 percent in Tamil Nadu, Goa, Himachal Pradesh, Maharashtra, Punjab and Kerala.

Health care experts have found that the elderly are highly prone to heart diseases, respiratory disorders, renal diseases, diabetes, hypertension, neurological problems and prostate issues.

"With limited resources, we need to adopt viable policy changes to manage the crisis of the aged."

The National Sample Survey Organisation calculates that one out of two elderly people in India suffers from at least one chronic disease, which requires lifelong medication.

The most recent data available, taken for the period 1995–96, revealed that 75 percent of aged individuals are affected by at least one disability relating to sight, hearing, speech, walking, and senility.

Dr. Shanthi Johnson, professor at the faculty of kinesiology and health studies at the Canada-based University of Regina, estimates that nearly eight percent of the elderly are immobile, while a disproportionately higher percentage of women are immobile compared to men.

"The average hospitalisation rate in the country per 100,000 aged persons is 7,633. There is considerable gender difference in the rate of hospitalisation, as a much greater proportion of men are hospitalised compared to their female counterparts," she added.

Nongovernmental organisations are advocating for more old-age homes, day care centers, physiotherapy clinics and temporary shelters for the rehabilitation of older persons, with government funds allocated to the running and maintaining of such projects.

Periodical and Internet Sources Bibliography

The following articles have been selected to supplement the diverse views presented in this chapter.

Advanta Home Care	"East vs. West: How We Treat Our Elderly," February 2, 2013. http://advantahomecare .net/east-vs-west-how-we-treat-our-elderly.
Firoozeh Mostafavi Darani et al.	"How Iranian Families Response to the Conditions Affecting Elderly Primary Health Care," *Research Journal of Biological Sciences*, vol. 5, no. 6, 2010.
Jill Insley	"Age Discrimination Ruling Allows Employers to Set Retirement Dates," *Guardian*, April 25, 2012.
Judy Lin	"Scholar Intrigued by How Societies Treat Their Elderly," *UCLA Today*, January 7, 2010.
Sarah McBride	"Special Report: Silicon Valley's Dirty Secret—Age Bias," Reuters, November 27, 2012. http://www.reuters.com/article/2012/11/27 /us-valley-ageism-idUSBRE8AQ0JK20121127.
Adam Minter	"In China, Don't Dare Help the Elderly," Bloomberg, September 8, 2011. http://www .bloomberg.com/news/2011-09-08/in-china -don-t-dare-help-the-elderly-adam-minter.html.
Sunanda Poduwal	"Age Discrimination: New Phenomenon Emerging at the Workplace," *Times of India*, July 24, 2011.
Ramona Tancau	"Norway in Top Three for Elderly Care," *The Foreigner*, May 26, 2011. http://theforeigner.no /pages/news/norway-in-top-three-for-elderly -care.

CHAPTER 4

Health Issues and Aging

Hungry, Thirsty, Unwashed: NHS Treatment of the Elderly Condemned

Jeremy Laurance

Jeremy Laurance is the health editor for the Independent. *In the following viewpoint, he reports on an investigation of ten cases of neglect by the British National Health Service (NHS). The cases revealed a lack of care and callousness, which Laurance links to ageism and indifference regarding the well-being of the elderly. Laurance reports that reforms and budget cuts at the NHS may worsen the situation further, and he concludes that a change of attitude toward the elderly is desperately needed at the NHS.*

As you read, consider the following questions:

1. Why were the ten patients mentioned in the report investigated?

2. What statistics does Laurance use to show that the ten elderly patients selected for review were not isolated cases?

3. What did the National Confidential Enquiry into Patient Outcome and Death find about older patients?

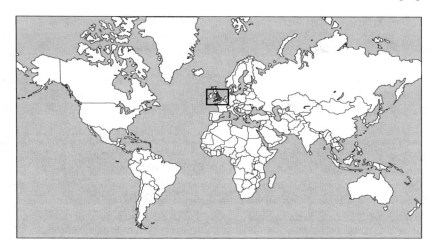

Elderly people treated by the NHS were denied even the most basic standards of care, according to a scathing report that reveals a health service rife with ageism.

Patients were left hungry and thirsty, unwashed, in soiled clothes, without adequate pain relief or an emergency call button in reach. Relatives were ignored or forgotten.

Investigations of 10 cases in which patients suffered unnecessary pain, indignity and distress while being looked after in hospital or by GPs, exposed a fundamental lack of humanity and compassion. The patients were selected from among 9,000 complaints to the Health Service Ombudsman. Nine of the 10 patients cited in the report died.

Patients were left hungry and thirsty, unwashed, in soiled clothes, without adequate pain relief or an emergency call button in reach.

The shocking catalogue exposes the gulf between the principles and values laid out in the NHS constitution and the reality of being an older person in the care of the health service today, said the Health Service Ombudsman, Ann Abraham. Her report comes after a decade of investigations that have revealed an NHS riddled with ageist attitudes, in which elderly patients are neglected, poorly treated and marginalised.

The cases in the Ombudsman's report include:

- A man with advanced stomach cancer who was discharged on the eve of a bank holiday from the Bolton NHS Trust with too little morphine to control his pain, leaving his family to drive around most of the weekend, frantically trying to obtain more supplies.

- A woman admitted to Ealing Hospital NHS Trust with breathing difficulties whose husband was left, forgotten, in a waiting room for three hours, denying him the chance to be with his wife when she died.

- A woman discharged from Heart of England NHS Trust to a care home who arrived bruised, soaked in urine, dishevelled and wearing someone else's clothes.

Shortage of money and resources was not the problem, Ms Abraham said, but rather it was an "ignominious failure" to look beyond a patient's clinical condition and respond to their social and emotional needs.

"The findings of my investigations reveal an attitude—both personal and institutional—which fails to recognise the humanity and individuality of the people concerned and to respond to them with sensitivity, compassion and professionalism. . . . The difficulties encountered by the service users and their relatives were not solely a result of illness, but arose from the dismissive attitude of staff, a disregard for process and procedure and an apparent indifference of NHS staff to deplorable standards of care."

The 10 patients selected for the report were "not isolated cases" she said. Of nearly 9,000 complaints to the Ombudsman last year, 18 per cent were about the care of elderly people and twice as many were accepted for investigation as for all other age groups put together.

Discriminatory attitudes towards the elderly in the NHS have been obvious for decades. The over-65s occupy almost two-thirds of hospital beds but despite a decade of rapidly increasing spending on the NHS, they still receive second-class care.

"The findings of my investigations reveal an attitude— both personal and institutional—which fails to recognise the humanity and individuality of the people concerned."

In 2006, a joint report by the former Healthcare Commission, Audit Commission and Commission for Social Inspection criticised the "patronising and thoughtless" manner in which NHS hospitals and care institutions treated older patients.

Last October, the National Confidential Enquiry into Patient Outcome and Death revealed that two out of three older patients admitted for emergency surgery received poor care with many left in pain. In December, the Patients Association published an investigation into 17 cases showing serious failings in hospital care from among hundreds it had received. Last month figures from the Office for National Statistics showed more than 1,000 patients died in hospital with dehydration or malnutrition.

As the coalition government prepares to launch the biggest reform in the NHS's history, managers have been told to find £20bn of savings and medical and nursing staff are being cut, which will reduce the time available for those who remain to provide basic care.

Ms Abraham said it was clear from her caseload that many patients were suffering in a similar way to the ten described in her report.

"The NHS must close the gap between the promise of care and compassion outlined in its constitution and the injustice that many older people experience," she said.

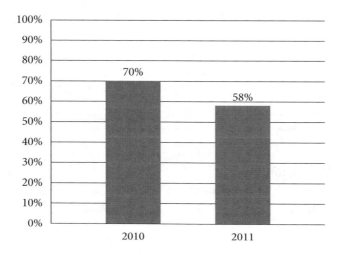

Percentage of Public Satisfied with How the National Health Service Is Run

TAKEN FROM: Kyrsty Hazell, "NHS: Biggest Drop in Satisfaction Since Eighties, Report Reveals," *Huffington Post*, December 6, 2012. www.huffingtonpost.co.uk.

Katherine Murphy, chief executive of the Patients Association said: "Yet another damning report confirming what we already know. How many reports do we have to have before anything will change?"

When Mrs H was transferred from Heart of England NHS Foundation Trust to a care home, she arrived bruised, soaked in urine, disheveled and wearing someone else's clothes.

Dr Peter Carter, Chief Executive of the Royal College of Nursing, said: "There can be no hiding place for inhumane treatment or poor care. The overwhelming majority of nurses will join us in condemning the failures outlined by the Ombudsman. However, we know that the NHS is expected to save up to £20bn in England alone, and with 27,000 posts already earmarked to be lost, it is inevitable that there will be an impact on front-line care. Last week, 80 per cent of RCN members surveyed told us that they did not have enough staff to deliver good quality care to patients."

The care services minister, Paul Burstow, said spot inspections by nurses and measures to improve patient involvement would hold local NHS services to account. "This report exposes the urgent need to update our NHS. We need a culture where poor practice is challenged and quality is the watchword. The coalition's plans will free front-line staff to focus on what matters most to patients and carers."

Case Studies

Mrs H's story: When Mrs H was transferred from Heart of England NHS Foundation Trust to a care home, she arrived bruised, soaked in urine, dishevelled and wearing someone else's clothes.

Mrs N's story: While doctors at Northern Lincolnshire and Goole Hospitals NHS Foundation Trust diagnosed Mrs N's lung cancer, they neglected to address the severe pain that she was suffering.

Mr W's story: The life of Mr W, who had dementia, was put at risk when Ashford and St Peter's Hospitals NHS Foundation Trust stopped treating him for pneumonia and dehydration and then discharged him to a care home on Christmas Eve. His life was saved by another hospital.

Mr C's story: Mr C died two hours after undergoing heart surgery at Oxford Radcliffe Hospitals NHS Trust. His family was not told that his condition had worsened and staff turned off his life support, despite his family's request to wait while they made a phone call.

Mr and Mrs J's story: Hospital staff at Ealing Hospital NHS Trust left Mr J forgotten in a waiting room, denying him the chance to be with his wife as she died.

Mrs R's story: Mrs R suffered nine falls while in Southampton University Hospitals NHS Trust but only one was recorded in the nursing notes. She was left with a big bruise on her face which distressed her family when viewing her body after she died. She was not offered a bath or shower during her 13-week admission, her family claim.

Mr L's story: Mr L had Parkinson's disease and was in a disturbed mental state when he was admitted to the Surrey and Borders Partnership NHS Foundation Trust and treated with excessive doses of an anti-psychotic drug. He developed pneumonia and died.

Mr D's story: Royal Bolton Hospital NHS Foundation Trust discharged Mr D with inadequate pain relief, leaving his family to find someone to dispense and administer morphine over a bank holiday weekend.

The AIDS Epidemic in Africa Has Robbed the Elderly of Vital Caretakers

Ruthann Richter

Ruthann Richter is media relations director at Stanford University School of Medicine. In the following viewpoint, she reports on a research project that looked into elders left alone when younger family members died of AIDS. The study found a substantial number of elderly who live without support of younger adults, often raising young children on their own. Richter concludes that orphaned elderly are a serious problem in Africa, and she says that governments and humanitarian organizations need to take such elders into account when allocating resources.

As you read, consider the following questions:

1. What does Grant Miller say he was unable to closely examine in his study?
2. Who did the Stanford survey cover, according to the viewpoint?
3. What elderly population does Tim Kautz say would not have been accounted for in the study?

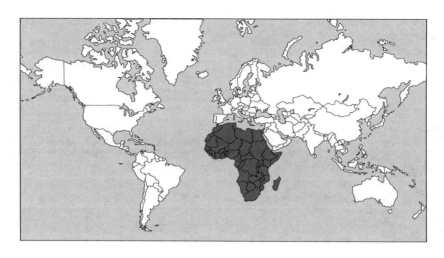

The rise in AIDS death rates in sub-Saharan Africa has led to a burgeoning new category of neglected individuals—nearly a million orphaned elderly, or older adults living alone without the benefit of any caregivers, Stanford University School of Medicine researchers have found.

A Missing Generation

The researchers used existing data to develop the first estimates on the number of elders left alone, without any adult support, as a result of the AIDS epidemic, said Grant Miller, PhD, MPP, assistant professor of medicine who is affiliated with the Stanford Center for Health Policy.

"We find that AIDS has produced close to a million elderly people in sub-Saharan Africa who are living without the support of their sons, daughters or other younger adults. Many of them also live with young children under 10 years of age, creating households with a missing generation of adults," said Miller, senior author of the study. "I think this probably understates the magnitude of the problem. We were unable to closely examine material living conditions or elderly health."

The study appears in the June 16 [2010] online issue of the *British Medical Journal*. Miller's coauthors at the Stanford

Center for Health Policy are Jay Bhattacharya, MD, PhD, associate professor of medicine, and Eran Bendavid, MD, instructor of medicine.

Miller said he and his colleagues were stunned to learn that no one had taken a systematic look at this potentially large group of needy individuals.

"It just blew me away," he said. "We all know we have this problem with orphaned children. I wondered, do we have a similar problem with orphaned elderly? I searched a variety of publications and didn't find a clear answer."

"We find that AIDS has produced close to a million elderly people in sub-Saharan Africa who are living without the support of their sons, daughters or other young adults."

Tim Kautz, the lead author of the study, said the idea for the project struck a chord with him, as he had spent a summer doing AIDS education in rural Tanzania. He lived there with a family that had taken in an unrelated, elderly villager who had no one else to look after him.

"I saw both the devastation caused by AIDS and the importance of the family in caring for the elderly. This project was a way to combine the two observations," said Kautz, a former Stanford undergraduate now pursuing a PhD in economics at the University of Chicago.

Neglected Elders

The researchers used data from the [MEASURE] Demographic and Health Surveys, a USAID [United States Agency for International Development]-funded database that provides standardized information on maternal/child health, HIV and other health indicators in low- and middle-income countries. The survey covered 123,000 individuals over age 60 living in 22 African countries between 1991 and 2006.

AIDS, Africa, and Poverty

A great many things made Africa particularly susceptible to AIDS, some of them innate to the communities where the disease flourished, and many others imposed from outside. The key factor is poverty. Put simply, millions of Africans are living with a virus from which they might easily have been protected if they had had access to education about it, or to the means of defending themselves. At the same time, their lack of resources led them to do things—to sell sex, to stay with a philandering husband, to leave their families and seek work far away—that they might not otherwise have done: This too spread the disease. And the destitution and weakness of many sub-Saharan states crippled their ability to respond once their populations were infected. [Democratic Republic of the] Congo didn't have the surveillance systems to detect or track the disease when it first emerged; Kenya didn't have the money to reach its populations with protective measures; Zambia didn't have the nurses or doctors to care for the sick; Lesotho couldn't buy the drugs that would have saved the dying.

Stephanie Nolen, 28: Stories of AIDS in Africa.
Toronto, Canada: Vintage Canada, 2008, p. 14.

The scientists found a very strong correlation between the rise in AIDS death rates in these countries and an increase in elderly individuals living alone. For every one-point increase in AIDS mortality rates, they found a 1.5 percent increase in elderly people left to manage on their own.

In the 22 countries, the estimates translated into 582,200 to 917,000 elderly people left unattended, the researchers found. About a third of them—or as many as 323,000—were also caring for young children. These individuals were more likely to be women, uneducated, living in rural areas and poorer than their attended counterparts. The results suggest HIV/AIDS has had a disproportionate impact on elderly people of lower socioeconomic status, the researchers reported.

Few African countries have public pension programs . . . most rely on traditional family structures, now undercut by the strain of AIDS.

Kautz said he was surprised the figures weren't even higher. He said he believes there are many more older individuals who have been left alone as their children die of AIDS, but that these elders have moved in with relatives or neighbors. These individuals would not be accounted for in the study, he said.

Although HIV has generally reduced life expectancies in Africa, those who escape the epidemic are living much longer as a result of greater access to health technologies, the researchers said. So there is an increased need for elder care services, they noted.

Yet few African countries have public pension programs or formal systems for caring for elders; most rely on traditional family structures, now undercut by the strain of AIDS, to provide this service. The researchers said the study points to the importance of taking these needy elders into consideration in allocating resources and planning programs.

"This is another component of the social consequences of HIV. So people in agencies who make resource allocation decisions need to consider this cost of HIV, and it's a pretty important one," Miller said. "Those working on the ground dealing with late-stage AIDS patients also need to think about the dependents of these patients."

Policies that help reduce AIDS mortality also will be of help to this group, he said.

"Future work is needed to more closely examine the health and overall welfare of this population, but our work suggests that reducing AIDS deaths in Africa may provide substantial benefits to this under-recognized population," the researchers concluded.

The researchers said the study is just a first step in understanding the problem. They speculate that elderly individuals who are alone suffer greater health problems, though they didn't specifically address the issue in the study. Similarly, they did not look at quality-of-life issues, though they suspect that these elders suffer physical and financial burdens as a result of being primary caregivers for young children. More research is needed on the health, well-being and other issues associated with these neglected elders, they said.

The study was funded by the National Institutes of Health.

Latin America's Aging Population Must Deal with Chronic Diseases

André C. Medici

André C. Medici is a senior health economist with the World Bank. In the following viewpoint, he looks at Latin America's aging population and the escalating problem of chronic diseases associated with that demographic. While discussing the financial and social impact of disease, Medici also looks into possible solutions such as creating a new health policy. He spends time detailing multiple diseases, their impact, and their treatment.

As you read, consider the following questions:

1. What implications, according to the viewpoint, would a new health policy agenda have on supply and demand?

2. What, in Medici's opinion, led the United States to have $7,290 per capita health expenditure?

3. According to the SABE survey, what percentage of the aging LAC population has diabetes?

Medici, André C. 2011. "How Age Influences the Demand for Health Care in Latin America," *Population Aging: Is Latin America Ready?* © World Bank, 2011. http://wwwwds.worldbank.org/external/default/WDSContentServer/WDSP/IB/2011/01/07/000356161_20110107011214/Rendered/PDF/588420PUB0Popu11public10BOX3538 16B0.pdf. License: Creative Commons Attribution CC BY 3.0.

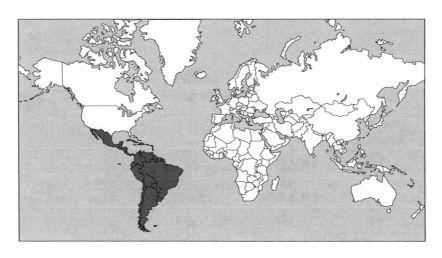

One of the most dramatic changes worldwide in the last 50 years is the population aging process, which is associated with the demographic effects of decreasing fertility and increasing life span. This process started early in developed countries and was followed in developing countries; however, the pace of the process accelerated in certain regions, including Latin America and the Caribbean (LAC). Population aging, when combined with other economic, labor market, health status, and health care trends, points to a number of socioeconomic and policy challenges in the decades ahead.

Disease and Aging in Latin America

The incidence of chronic diseases increases with aging, as does the number of medical visits, medicines consumed, and hospitalizations, with great impact on the aging adult's family budget. The health care costs for people age 65 and older are several times greater than the cost for young people in many developed countries, and chronic diseases disproportionately affect older adults and are associated with disability and diminished quality of life.

Demographic changes associated with aging demand a new health policy agenda, with implications for the supply and demand sides. On the supply side, the biggest challenge is how to face the fiscal impacts of aging in order to provide funds to finance more and expensive health services. On the demand side, the challenge is to implement policy measures to promote healthy behaviors and other preventive actions among older adults, and to achieve affordable costs for health insurance plans, drugs, and medical procedures.

Despite these challenges, poor health is not an inevitable consequence of aging. Many successful policies to prevent diseases and disabilities in developed countries are providing better coverage and quality of health care to the aging. Controlling risk factors such as high blood pressure, obesity, and diabetes, and promoting healthy behaviors by reducing smoking, alcohol consumption, and a sedentary lifestyle, could help prevent the early consequences of chronic diseases in older adults. Public health interventions could help stem the rising costs of health care by promoting the use of effective preventive measures to make healthy aging a reality.

The health care costs for people age 65 and older are several times greater than the cost for young people in many developed countries.

The social and economic circumstances of the aging, such as late retirement, improvement of health and functional ability, and public and private policies that influence individual well-being are in a state of continuing evolution and transition. Understanding the complexities of this situation and the relationship among demographics, policy, social behavior, economics, and health is essential to improve the design of social policies and to guarantee a better quality of life for the aging.

Aging and Chronic Diseases

Chronic diseases disproportionately affect older adults and are associated with disability and diminished quality of life. They are often associated with increasing health care facility needs and expensive long-term-care costs. These facts have been known for a long time. . . .

The natural aging of the population increases the weight of chronic health conditions in the BOD [burden of disease, a rough measure of mortality and illness], but the high impact of chronic diseases on health costs, which was accepted as a given in past decades, has become increasingly controversial in recent years. In fact, chronic diseases—differently from acute health episodes—undermine a long and continuous process of using health facilities and spending on medicines, exams, and medical visits. Health conditions such as stroke, heart disease, fractures and osteoporosis, Alzheimer's [disease], and the results of diabetes such as blindness and amputations increase with the aging process and their treatment and use of health facilities is continuous and expensive. Frequently, the high technology used in treatment and medical exams and the consumption of expensive medicines by the aging are singled out as a major factor leading to higher health expenditures during the aging process. It creates a stepwise effect in the health expenditure curve by age, which is often considered in future budgetary estimations based on demographic forecasting.

Living Healthier and Longer

However, a new debate is behind these arguments. Many policy makers and governmental agencies, such as the Centers for Disease Control [and Prevention] (CDC) in the United States, maintain that health systems centered on the use of medical technology, without sound health promotion and prevention policies, tend to spend more on health care during the aging process without achieving good outcomes. A better integration among public health, preventive care, and less aggressive treatments should enable the older population to live longer, more healthy lives with lower personal and institutional health spending. In the United States, for example, the intensive use of medical technology, especially for treatments associated with old age, is one of the factors that led to a per capita health expenditure of US$7,290 in 2007 compared with US$3,601 in France, US$3,588 in Germany, and US$2,992 in the United Kingdom. However, life expectancy at birth in the United States in 2007 was behind these countries: 78.1 years, compared with 79.5 years in the United Kingdom, 80.0 years in Germany, and 81.0 years in France.

Many policy makers and governmental agencies . . . maintain that health systems centered on the use of medical technology, without sound health promotion and prevention policies, tend to spend more on health care during the aging process without achieving good outcomes.

The increasing prevalence of chronic diseases in an aged population also implies a higher burden of disability. Information about old-age disability as a consequence of chronic diseases has been collected in seven Latin America and the Caribbean cities (Buenos Aires, Bridgetown, Havana, Mexico City, Montevideo, São Paulo, and Santiago) by the Survey on Health, Well-Being, and Aging in Latin America and the Caribbean (*Salud, Bienestar y Envejecimiento en America Latina y el Caribe*, SABE). According to the survey, for all considered cities, only 20.7 percent of the population aged 60 and older declared they were in good health during 1999–2000. . . .

Most of the aging (77 percent) according to the SABE survey live with disease, and a considerable proportion of this population (44 percent) has comorbidities [additional diseases in addition to a primary disease].

Nineteen percent of the population claim to have disabilities, and a larger proportion of the aging lives with the combined effects of disability and disease (17 percent) and disability and comorbidity (12 percent). This indicates that disability

Prevalence of Diseases or Chronic Conditions in Latin America and the Caribbean

Diseases or Chronic Conditions	Prevalence %
Hypertension (high blood pressure)	48.1
Arthritis	40.1
Heart disease (cardiovascular disease)	19.3
Diabetes	15.9
Lung disease	9.9
Stroke	5.9
Cancer	4.0

SABE, Survey on Health, Well-Being, and Aging in Latin America and the Caribbean, 1999–2000.

TAKEN FROM: André C. Medici, "How Age Influences the Demand for Health Care in Latin America," in *Population Aging: Is Latin America Ready?* Ed. Daniel Cotlear. Washington, DC: World Bank, 2011, p. 149.

in old age is mostly a consequence of chronic diseases and co-morbidities, and the prevention of risk factors that lead to chronic conditions could reduce the burden of disability in the aging, resulting in increased quality of life and reduced health expenditures along the aging process.

Some governmental agencies, such as the CDC, argue, based on research reviews, that health promotion activities, such as education and counseling interventions, could improve preventive health behaviors among the aging. Although these studies focused on prevention in healthy people, there is an increasing consensus that behavioral techniques such as self-monitoring, personal communication with health care providers, and viewing audiovisual materials contribute to successful change in behaviors such as quitting smoking, controlling alcohol consumption, improving nutrition, and weight control.

Hypertension

The SABE survey also shows that seven diseases and chronic conditions disproportionately affect the health status of the population aged 60 and older in LAC.

Hypertension (high blood pressure) is more a chronic condition than a disease. It is more common in men, and women are more likely to develop high blood pressure after menopause. Hypertension could lead to several other chronic conditions such as heart disease and kidney failure. Hypertension has the highest prevalence compared with other chronic conditions among elders in the seven cities surveyed.

There is an increasing consensus that behavioral techniques such as self-monitoring, personal communication with health care providers, and viewing audiovisual materials contribute to successful change in behaviors.

Almost half of the population aged 60 and older has hypertension. São Paulo has the highest prevalence (54 percent) and Mexico City the lowest (43 percent). Despite that, hypertension appears to have less association with disability for the aging than other chronic conditions such as arthritis. In fact, many studies, as related by [M.G.] Lima and others (2009), reveal that hypertension can have a long and asymptomatic progression, with no great impact on the quality of life of patients, despite the fact that it affects a large number of aging individuals.

Relevant risk factors linked to hypertension are obesity and being overweight, followed by the absence of physical activity, tobacco use, and diet, including the overconsumption of sodium and alcohol and low potassium and vitamin D. Stress and other chronic comorbidities, such as high cholesterol, diabetes, and kidney failure, also contribute to increasing blood pressure.

Obesity and Arthritis

Obesity is the highest risk factor for hypertension but also for other chronic conditions such as type 2 diabetes. Risks associated with hypertension are early mortality by stroke, heart disease, and certain kinds of cancers. [M.V.] Andrade (2006), using SABE survey data, pointed out that the current levels of obesity in LAC appear to be very high, especially for women. Current levels of obesity among the aging require changes in lifestyle and diet, and increases in physical activity, but in many cases professional help is necessary to reduce body weight. Some studies developed on the basis of other surveys demonstrated that hypertension was more prevalent among the poor and less educated population. This fact changes the traditional perception that correlates poverty with communicable diseases in LAC. It also shows how important it is to tackle chronic conditions as a way to reduce poverty in the region.

Arthritis is an inflammation of one or more joints, such as the knee, wrist, or spinal column. The two most common types of arthritis are osteoarthritis and rheumatoid arthritis. Joint pain and stiffness are the main symptoms of this disease. Rheumatoid arthritis is primarily a bone and joint disease, but it occasionally damages other parts of the body, including the eyes and lungs.

Arthritis is ranked the second-most-common highly prevalent chronic condition or disease in the seven LAC cities surveyed. Forty percent of the population aged 60 and older has arthritis. A higher prevalence was found in Havana (56 percent) and a lower prevalence was found in Mexico City (25 percent). Self-reported pain among people with arthritis across all countries ranged from 30.7 percent in older Mexican Americans to 83.7 percent in Santiago. Arthritis is more prevalent among aging women and its risk factors are associated with family history and smoking. Arthritis causes other problems among which is joint damage that can be both debilitating and disfiguring, making it difficult or impossible to perform daily activities.

Heart Disease and Diabetes

Heart disease (cardiovascular disease, CVD) is a broad term used to describe a range of diseases that affect heart conditions, and in some cases, blood vessels. The various diseases that fall under the umbrella of heart disease include diseases of blood vessels, such as coronary artery disease; heart rhythm problems (arrhythmias); and congenital heart defects. Heart disease is prevalent in 19 percent of the aging in the seven LAC cities surveyed. The highest rates of CVD were found in Santiago (32 percent) and the lowest in Mexico City (10 percent). The risk factors for CVD are the same for men and women. They include inactivity, overweight and obesity, poor diet and nutrition, smoking, high blood pressure, high blood cholesterol, and diabetes. The most common consequences of CVD are heart attack and stroke.

The population of Latin America has remarkably higher proportions of abdominal obesity, high blood cholesterol, and hypertension, according to the results of a study published in the March 6, 2007, edition of the American Heart Association's journal, *Circulation*. The study analyzed data from the six Latin American countries that participated in the INTER-HEART international study. In Argentina, Brazil, Chile, Colombia, Guatemala, and Mexico, the population-adjusted risk for abdominal obesity was 48.6 percent compared to 31.2 percent in the 46 other countries that participated in INTER-HEART. For high blood cholesterol, the risk was 42 percent compared to 32 percent in the other countries. For hypertension, the risk was 29.1 percent compared to 20.8 percent in the other countries. At 48.1 percent, the population-adjusted risk for tobacco smoking was about the same for both the Latin American and the non–Latin American countries.

Diabetes is a condition in which the body either does not produce enough, or does not properly respond to, insulin, a hormone produced in the pancreas. Insulin enables cells to absorb glucose in order to turn it into energy. A malfunction in this ability causes glucose to accumulate in the blood, leading to various potential complications, among them the risk of heart attack, stroke, blindness, kidney failure, and gangrene. The two types of diabetes are type 1 (failure to produce insulin) and type 2 (insulin resistance). The latter is commonly associated with aging.

Arthritis is ranked the second-most-common highly prevalent chronic condition or disease in the seven LAC cities surveyed.

The SABE survey estimates that 16 percent of the aging LAC population has diabetes. Higher scores were found in Bridgetown (22 percent) and lower scores were found in Buenos Aires (12 percent). Consistent with other studies, older adults with less than three years of education were twice as likely to report having diabetes as other older adults, showing a strong correlation between diabetes and poverty among older people. The study also reveals that in the group aged 60–74, among those reporting diabetes, at least 60 percent also reported problems seeing well with or without eyeglasses, and 20 percent had difficulty with at least one activity of daily living (ADL). In the nondiabetic group of the same age group, only 13 percent reported difficulties with ADLs.

Lung Disease and Stroke

Chronic lung disease (chronic obstructive pulmonary disease, COPD) is a group of progressive respiratory disorders with diffuse abnormalities of gas transport and exchange. The aging are subject to COPD due not only to the biological process of aging, which includes decreased pulmonary tissue elasticity, but also to prolonged exposure to pollutants or occupational environment. Cigarette smoking is a major factor in the development of COPD. Environmental exposure to sulfur dioxide, asbestos, and cotton dust are causative factors that predispose the respiratory tract to chronic infection. Repeated pulmonary infections can result in the alteration of lung structure and the destruction of pulmonary tissue. The disease is more prevalent in men than in women.

According to the SABE survey, 10 percent of the population aged 60 and older reported it had COPD, varying from 13 percent (Havana) to 4 percent (Bridgetown) in the seven cities surveyed. The Latin American Project for the Investigation of Obstructive Lung Disease examined the prevalence of post-bronchodilator airflow limitation (Stage I: Mild COPD and higher) among people over age 40 in five major Latin American cities, each in a different country—Brazil, Chile, Mexico, Uruguay, and República Bolivariana de Venezuela. In each country, the prevalence of Stage I: Mild COPD and higher increased steeply with age, with the highest prevalence among those over age 60, ranging from a low of 18.4 percent in Mexico City, Mexico, to a high of 32.1 percent in Montevideo, Uruguay. In all cities/countries, the prevalence was appreciably higher in men than in women.

Stroke (cerebrovascular disease) occurs when the blood supply to a part of the brain is interrupted or severely reduced, depriving brain tissue of oxygen and nutrients. Within a few minutes, brain cells begin to die. Stroke is a medical emergency, and prompt treatment is crucial. Early treatment can minimize brain damage and potential stroke complications. Strokes can be treated, and a much smaller number of people in high-income countries die of stroke than 20 or 30 years ago. Improvement in the control of major risk factors for stroke—high blood pressure, smoking, and high cholesterol—is likely responsible for the decline. Stroke is one of the leading disability factors in the aging.

On average, 6 percent of the aging in LAC suffer a stroke, varying from 4 percent in Montevideo to 10 percent in Havana, among the seven surveyed cities. According to [P.M.] Lavados and others (2007), stroke mortality in LAC is higher than in developed countries, but rates are declining. Population-based studies show variations in incidence of stroke—lower rates of ischemic stroke and similar rates of intracranial hemorrhage compared with other regions. A significant proportion of strokes in these populations can be attributed to a few preventable risk factors. Some countries have published national clinical guidelines, although much needs to be done in the organization of care and rehabilitation. Even though the burden of stroke is high, there is a paucity of information for implementing evidence-based management.

Cancer

Cancer is a class of diseases in which a group of cells display uncontrolled growth (division beyond the normal limits), invasion (intrusion into and destruction of adjacent tissues), and sometimes metastasis (spread to other locations in the body via the lymph system or blood). Cancer affects people at all ages with the risk for most types increasing with age. Cancer caused about 13 percent of human deaths worldwide in 2007 (7.6 million). According to [J.] Hansen (1998), based on data from cancer registries in 51 countries on five continents, contrary to the pattern in younger age groups, in which annual cancer rates are almost equally distributed between both genders, aging men have twice the cancer incidence rate as aging women. For all major specific cancer sites except testicular cancer, the incidence rate is significantly higher among the aging than among any groups of younger and middle-aged persons. Among aging men, the most common kinds of cancer are prostate, lung, and colon cancers, and among aging women they are breast, colon, lung, and stomach cancers.

According to the SABE survey, cancer has a prevalence of 4 percent in the seven LAC cities surveyed, varying from 2 percent in Mexico City to 6 percent in Montevideo. Although cancer in the aging is extremely common, few oncology health professionals are familiar with caring for some kinds of cancer in senior patients. Surgery is at present the first choice but is frequently delivered in a suboptimal way, with a huge range of poorly tested protocols. In some cases, undertreatment is justified by concerns about unsustainable toxicity, while overtreatment is explained by the lack of knowledge about optimizing preoperative risk assessment.

Health Issues Plague the Aging Prison Population in the United States

James Ridgeway

James Ridgeway is a former senior correspondent at Mother Jones *and a 2012 Soros Justice Media Fellow. In the following viewpoint, he reports that the number of elderly prison inmates is rising rapidly in US prisons. Many of these inmates have serious medical conditions, and there are few facilities in prison to deal with them. He argues that keeping men over fifty-five and sixty-five in prison makes little sense since they are unlikely to commit new crimes. In addition, he says it is expensive and inhumane, since they cannot receive proper care.*

As you read, consider the following questions:

1. How many prisoners over fifty-five and sixty-five were housed in US prisons as of 2010?
2. What data from New York State suggests that older prisoners are unlikely to re-offend?
3. What does Jack Donson say are the shortcomings of the elderly offender pilot program?

James Ridgeway, "The Other Death Sentence," *Mother Jones*, September 25, 2012. © 2012, Foundation for National Progress.

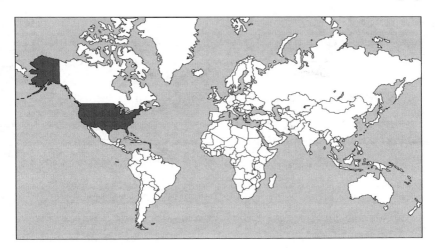

William "Lefty" Gilday had been in prison 40 years when the dementia began to set in. At 82, he was already suffering from advanced Parkinson's disease and a host of other ailments, and his friends at MCI [Massachusetts Correctional Institution] Shirley, a medium security prison in Massachusetts, tried to take care of him as best they could. Most of them were aging lifers like Lefty, facing the prospect of one day dying behind bars themselves, so they formed an ad hoc hospice team in their crowded ward. They bought special food from the commissary, heated it in an ancient microwave, and fed it to their friend. They helped him to the toilet and cleaned him up. Joe Labriola, 64, tried to see that Lefty got a little sunshine every day, wheeling his chair out into the yard and sitting with his arm around him to keep him from falling out.

"We Loved the Old Man"

But Lefty, who was serving life without parole for killing a police officer during a failed bank heist in 1970, slipped ever deeper into dementia. One day he threw an empty milk carton at a guard and was placed in a "medical bubble," a kind of solitary confinement unit with a glass window that enables health care staffers to keep an eye on the prisoner. His friends were denied entrance, but Joe managed to slip in one day. He recalls an overpowering stench . . . and a stack of unopened food containers—Lefty explained that he couldn't open the tabs. Joe also noticed that the nurses in the adjoining observation room had blocked the glass with manila folders so they wouldn't have to look at the old man.

Lefty had been popular among the prisoners, though. A minor-league ballplayer turned 1960s radical—his southpaw, not his politics, earned him the nickname—he was the subject of one of the most infamous manhunts in Massachusetts history. He had already been in and out of prison several times on robbery offenses when he fell in with a group of Brandeis University students who decided that stealing guns and money could help them foment a black revolution. They held up a bank in 1970, and when Boston police responded, guns drawn, a patrolman named Walter Schroeder was shot dead. Lefty claimed that he never meant to shoot the guy—that it was a warning round that ricocheted—but the jury didn't buy it, and he was convicted of first-degree murder and sentenced to death. (The students got no more than seven years.)

In 1972, after the Supreme Court briefly banned capital punishment, Lefty became a lifer. Over time, he also became a jailhouse lawyer—an inmate paralegal who puts together legal cases for fellow prisoners—settling disputes and eventually gaining a rep as something of an elder statesman. When Lefty died last September [in 2011], his friends were denied permission to hold a memorial service in the prison chapel, so they ended up holding it in a classroom. The service culminated in some 80 men sailing paper planes into the air as a tribute. "We loved the old man," Joe Labriola wrote me in a letter.

Lefty Gilday was no ordinary inmate, but in one regard he typified a growing segment of America's inmate population— geriatric prisoners. The United States leads the world in incarceration, with more than 2.2 million people in its prisons and jails, and the graying of this population is shaping up to be a crisis with moral, practical, and economic implications for cash-strapped governments. In recent years, a growing number of advocates—and even a handful of corrections officials and politicians—have dared to suggest that we consider setting some of these old-timers free.

Growing Older in Jail

As of 2010, state and federal prisons housed more than 26,000 inmates 65 and older and nearly five times that number 55 and up, according to a recent Human Rights Watch report. (Both numbers are significant, since long-term incarceration is said to add 10 years to a person's physical age; in prison, 55 is old.) From 1995 to 2010, as America's prison population grew 42 percent, the number of inmates over 55 grew at nearly seven times that rate. Today, roughly 1 in 12 state and federal prison inmates is 55 or older.

The trend is worsening. A new report from the American Civil Liberties Union [ACLU] estimates that, by 2030, the over-55 group will number more than 400,000—about a third of the overall prison population. "It's huge," says Bob Hood, the former warden of the mammoth federal correctional complex in Florence, Colorado. "We're behind the eight ball on this."

The United States leads the world in incarceration, with more than 2.2 million people in its prisons and jails.

The boom in geriatric prisoners is the inevitable result of legislation from the tough-on-crime 1980s and 1990s, which extended sentences and slashed parole opportunities, both dramatically so. According to a June report by the Pew Center on the States, drug offenders released in 2009 had spent 36 percent longer behind bars, on average, than those released in 1990. One in ten state prisoners nowadays is a lifer, and about the same proportion of federal prisoners over 50 are serving

30 to life. In short, more than 100,000 prisoners are currently destined to die in prison, and far more will remain there well into their 60s and 70s. Many of these men—as most of them are men—were never violent criminals, even in their youth. In Texas, for example, 65 percent of the older prisoners are in for nonviolent acts such as drug possession and property crimes.

Dropping Risk

Keeping thousands of old men locked away might make sense to diehards seeking maximum retribution or politicians seeking political cover, but it has little effect on public safety. By age 50, people are far less likely to commit serious crimes. "Arrest rates drop to 2 percent," explains Hood, the retired federal warden. "They are almost nil at the age of 65." The arrest rate for 16- to 19-year-olds, by contrast, runs around 12 percent.

Once released, therefore, the vast majority of the older prisoners never return. Data from New York State, for example, tracked 469 inmates who were originally sentenced for violent crimes and were later released as senior citizens—over a 13-year period, just 8 of those former inmates went back to prison, and only 1 went back for a violent offense. "The mass incarceration of the elderly is an example of our criminal justice system at its most heartless and its most irrational," says David Fathi, director of the ACLU's National Prison Project. "Most such prisoners are long past their crime-prone years and pose little to no public safety risk."

Beyond any questions of efficacy or mercy lies the looming issue of the price tag. According to the ACLU, caring for aging prisoners costs American taxpayers some $16 billion annually. We shell out roughly $68,000 a year for each inmate over 50, twice what it costs to keep a younger person locked up. And the older the inmate, the greater the cost. "I've had inmates where a total cost of $100,000 a year is on the low side," Hood says.

Even when you factor in post-incarceration expenses—for parole, housing, and public benefits such as health care—the ACLU projects that taxpayers save $66,000 a year, on average, for each inmate over 50 our prisons set free. "States are confronting the complex, expensive repercussions of their sentencing practices," notes a 2010 report from the Vera Institute of Justice.

Keeping thousands of old men locked away might make sense to diehards seeking maximum retribution or politicians seeking political cover, but it has little effect on public safety.

Soaring Medical Costs

It's not difficult to see why it costs so much. "The medical conditions that present themselves to long-term elderly inmates run anywhere from dialysis to cardiac treatment to dementia," says Carl ToersBijns, who worked his way up from guard to deputy warden during his 30 years in the New Mexico and Arizona prison systems. "It is staff intensive," he says. And the number of elderly inmates "is outgrowing the ability of corrections officers to handle and manage them—they're not medically trained."

Nor are prison facilities designed for people with mobility problems. Their assisted-living and hospice units are often chock full, Hood says, leaving the unlucky elders stuck in the general population without the services they need. Unless states start releasing them, Hood says, we will need to "retrofit every prison in America to put assisted-living units in it, wheelchair accessibility, handicapped toilets, grab bars—the whole nine yards."

In recent months, I have been corresponding with several older men in Massachusetts state prisons, and have visited one of them in person. They are all lifers with murder convictions, which makes them atypical even among the long-termers. These men will never be paroled, and they are unlikely to qualify for early release no matter how rehabilitated they might be or how aged and decrepit they become. They have accepted this, and have generally tried to make something of their lives in prison—serving as jailhouse lawyers, organizing against abusive conditions, and helping their friends survive.

"The medical conditions that present themselves to long-term elderly inmates run anywhere from dialysis to cardiac treatment to dementia."

I am 75, so we share a camaraderie of sorts as we compare notes on our aches and pains and medication regimens. They know I understand what it's like to be getting old and facing illness and death. They also know I have no idea what it's like to deal with these things behind bars. Their letters tell of lives filled with daily indignities—trying to heave an aging body into the top bunk, struggling to move fast enough to get a food tray filled or get a book at the library, fighting off younger troublemakers. But worst of all is the pervasive nothingness and isolation.

Prison officials tend to discourage close friendships, and they dislike anything that smacks of organizing, which is considered a security threat. So they routinely transfer inmates between prisons and deny them the right to communicate with friends in other facilities. The activities available—which are few, since lawmakers wiped out most rehabilitative programming during the 1980s and 1990s—are accessible only to inmates who can walk long prison hallways or climb stairs. For some old-timers, a cell is their entire world; doing time simply means awaiting death.

Little Help for the Old

Joe Labriola is a former Marine combat hero. Now 66, he joined the Marines at 17 and served two tours in Vietnam, receiving a Purple Heart and Bronze Star with Combat "V" for valor. After returning home, he was convicted of killing a drug dealer who was an FBI informant and got life without parole. So far he has served 38 years—18 in solitary.

Labriola has chronic breathing problems that he attributes to Agent Orange exposure. He says it's hard for him to walk more than 10 steps without help from an oxygen machine, so he's in a wheelchair a lot of the time. At least 75 prisons in 40 states now have hospices, but you won't find any in Massachusetts. At MCI Shirley, Labriola lives in a ward called Assisted Daily Living, which he describes in his letters as a clutch of hospital beds in a corridor. "We live in an 11-man ward with all the beds side by side," he says. "No ventilation or windows that can open. We do have hospital beds and standing wall lockers, something the general population does not have." Unlike most assisted-living facilities, this setup provides little actual assistance, he says, other than what "the prisoners who clean the floor and bathrooms render us when we ask." Residents get to move around outside the ward for just 10 minutes every hour, which means the person pushing Joe's wheelchair must race from place to place—the prison library, he estimates, is a quarter mile away.

For some old-timers, a cell is their entire world; doing time simply means awaiting death.

From his window, Labriola has a view of the prison hospital. "I see men coming up for medication and insulin at least three to four times per day," he says. "They come in chairs, Canadian canes, geriatric walkers. In one week alone we had three deaths." The hospital's inpatient facilities consist of a series of five small wards with five beds in each. Men in various stages of bad health or terminal illness lie in bed all day long with nothing to do but watch soap operas. "What they need is mental, spiritual, and human stimulation in the form of a one-to-one care provided by trained prisoners who would be first cleared for drug usage and sex crimes as there are female nurses in the area," Labriola suggests in one of his letters. "There are many men willing to volunteer their time and energies into making this a reality."

Lifer John Feroli told the following story in one of his letters: "A guy in his 70s I knew personally was in the [solitary confinement] unit because he failed to stand for the afternoon count. He was on the third floor of the housing unit, he was partially paralyzed from a stroke and the batteries in his hearing aid were dead and he never heard the announcement for Count Time."

The End of Parole

Another convicted murderer, 73-year-old Billy Barnoski, wrote me in April to report that he was in solitary after a younger cellmate jumped him and beat him up. His friends came to his aid, there was a melee, and four people were thrown in the hole. Barnoski suffers from a heart condition called atrial fibrillation, which is treated with a blood thinner called Coumadin. He also has high blood pressure, high cholesterol, shingles, and severe arthritis in his back and neck. He takes 25 pills daily. "There have been many times, so many, that they simply say, 'We haven't got that med today,'" he writes. "Mind you it has been heart meds just last week. Locked in this hole without necessary meds is torture."

Then there's Frank Soffen, also 73. Sentenced to life for second-degree murder, he has spent more than half of his life in prison. Nowadays he is confined to a wheelchair. He has kidney and liver disease and has suffered four heart attacks. He currently stays in the assisted living wing of Massachusetts' Norfolk prison. And because of his failing health and his clean record during 40 years behind bars—which included rescuing a guard being threatened by other prisoners—he has been held up as a candidate for compassionate release.

A Right to Care

Incarcerated men and women have a constitutional right to health care. International human rights law also mandates that persons deprived of their liberty receive health care. Older prisoners are at least two to three times as expensive to incarcerate as younger prisoners, primarily because of their greater medical needs. Our research shows prison medical expenditures for older inmates range from three to nine times higher than those for the average inmate.

The prevalence of illness and disability increases with age in prison, as in the community. The challenge for correctional systems is not only to provide for current needs, but to ensure projected needs can be met in the future. As the Tennessee Department of Correction noted:

[E]ven if the rate of growth of the elderly is only moderate, any anticipated growth in this population requires appropriate planning due to the resources required to meet their additional needs (additional medical staff, pharmaceuticals, medical equipment and treatment, etc.).

Human Rights Watch, "Old Behind Bars:
The Aging Prison Population in the United States," January 27, 2012.

Soffen is physically incapable of committing a violent crime. He cannot even hold a pen, in fact, so I had to rely on the other prisoners' accounts of his situation. They told me he has already participated in prerelease and furlough programs, and has a supportive family and a place to live with his son. One member of the state parole board recommended his release. But the board has denied him parole twice—in 2006 and again in January 2011. He won't be eligible for review for another five years—if he lives that long. These days he's warehoused in a medical observation bubble, bedridden, clad in adult diapers, unable to wash.

Gordon Haas, 68, is in better health, but he too has been in prison the better part of four decades, ever since his 1975 conviction for murdering his wife and children. While inside, Haas earned a master's degree from Boston University, but such opportunities are exceedingly rare nowadays. Ever since Willie Horton—the furloughed Massachusetts prisoner who went AWOL and committed murder only to become the bane of [former Massachusetts governor] Michael Dukakis' 1988 failed presidential run—Haas has witnessed the rollback of parole and the end of programs that once allowed inmates to work outside prison gates and further themselves on the inside.

The Old Are Growing Fast

This past May, I visited Haas at Norfolk prison, about 45 minutes outside Boston. Norfolk was designed for 750 men and holds 1,500. Built during the 1920s to mimic a college campus, its buildings look more like dormitories than cell blocks, if you ignore the razor wire.

Haas tells me his advocacy for prison reform has earned him the scrutiny of the prison's Inner Perimeter Security force, an internal police unit. They read his letters, he says, and monitor his phone calls. So rather than make a formal media request, I simply go in as a regular visitor.

Once I pass through the metal detectors—presenting ID, taking off my shoes and showing the bottoms of my feet, the underside of my collar, and the inside of my waistband—I proceed across the campus into a large visiting room filled with rows of chairs. Prisoners and visitors may sit next to, but not opposite, one another. They must keep their feet flat on the floor at all times and their backs against the chair backs. Guards posted at stations at either end of the room roam about and escort visitors to the toilet. Prisoners are strip-searched before they enter and after they leave.

Haas enters wearing a short-sleeve button down, pressed blue jeans, and thick glasses. With his neatly combed gray hair, he reminds me of an IBM executive on a visit to the factory floor. He is affable, and a keen storyteller. In addition to leading the Lifers Group, a collection of men unlikely to ever get out, Haas is chairman of the Store & Finance Committee of the Norfolk Inmate Council. He takes a big interest in Project Youth, which teaches younger prisoners to speak to students and youth groups about what led them to prison.

As of June, according to its own figures, the Massachusetts Department of Correction [DOC] had 11,679 inmates. About 19 percent of them were 50 or older and 6 percent were at least 60. Last year, Haas used the DOC's figures to produce his own report, which notes that the 60-plus contingent is the fastest-growing demographic in the state's prisons.

Haas says he has been urging the state to adopt a hospice program for more than 15 years. "Our contention is that since lifers will probably be in need of such care, we are a resource for others now," he says. But "the DOC does not sanction prisoners helping other prisoners. There is one outlet, and that is prisoners can volunteer to take those who can go outside out for programs and fresh air, even those in wheelchairs. That is good, but it is all there is."

The DOC confirms that it has neither prison hospices nor immediate plans to build any. By 2020, according to the state's DOC Master Plan, Massachusetts will need three "new specialized facilities" to house an estimated 1,270 prisoners with medical or mental health issues that would preclude them being housed in "regular" prisons. "We don't have a position on compassionate, geriatric, or any other type of release," a DOC spokeswoman told me via email. "That's up to the legislature." And while Massachusetts legislators have introduced a bill "establishing criteria for the compassionate release of terminally ill inmates," it has yet to make it past the "study" stage.

Geriatric Release

By 2010, according to the Vera Institute, 15 states and DC had approved some form of "geriatric release," while others had medical- or compassionate-release programs that could potentially apply to frail, aging prisoners. But "the jurisdictions are rarely using these provisions," its report notes, thanks to fearful politicians, a less-than-sympathetic public, narrow eligibility criteria, and red tape that discourages inmates from applying and can draw out the process indefinitely. Nobody has aggregated the state-to-state data, but it appears that the number of prisoners released under these programs totals no more than a few hundred.

Jack Donson, who spent 23 years as a case manager for the Federal Bureau of Prisons, points to the shortcomings of the elderly offender pilot program, part of 2008 federal legislation called the Second Chance Act. The law made the criteria for early release so strict, and the paperwork so extensive, Donson says, that it applied to only a few dozen inmates nationally. "I actually referred the first offender in the country" to the program, he notes on his website. "The bureaucrats deemed this offender dangerous to the community," because of a record of violence 30 years earlier, "yet he had been incarcerated in a camp setting (without a fence), was a model inmate with an outstanding work ethic who even participated in unescorted medical furloughs in the community."

The DOC [Department of Correction] confirms that it has neither prison hospices nor immediate plans to build any.

Little has changed in the interim. But Hood believes America is approaching a politically expedient moment. "You spend $68,000 to watch an inmate who is truly hospital-bound? I think most people would get that. They would understand that if there's another way to do it—let's do it outside the prison," he says. "Sixteen billion a year. Think about that number. It has to wake up some people."

"States just can't support the burden anymore," agrees former state warden Carl ToersBijns. "The only solution will be to release them or to ignore them." If we choose the latter, he cautions, prison death rates will skyrocket.

Of course, ignoring elderly prisoners *after* release could be just as devastating. The ACLU's Fathi emphasizes that institutionalized old folks will require plenty of help transitioning back into the community and getting the services they need. "For many elderly prisoners," he says, "particularly those with serious medical needs, simply pushing them out the prison door will be tantamount to a death sentence."

Indonesia Should Subsidize Immunizations for the Elderly

Lance Jennings

Lance Jennings is chairman of the Asia-Pacific Alliance for the Control of Influenza. In the following viewpoint, he says that Indonesia does a poor job of immunizing the elderly against influenza. Indonesia has one of the oldest populations in the world, therefore, the failure to immunize the elderly results in many avoidable deaths and illnesses, as well as in economic loss. Jennings argues that the Indonesian government needs to start providing free or subsidized vaccination and to educate the public about the dangers of the flu and the benefits of vaccination.

As you read, consider the following questions:

1. By how much does the influenza vaccine reduce the results of flu, according to World Health Organization statistics?

2. What are the levels of immunization of countries in the Asian region?

3. Why does Jennings conclude that the challenge of immunizing the elderly in Indonesia is not going to go away?

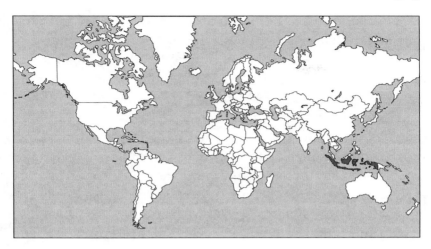

Indonesia has the fifth largest elderly population in the world, with 18 million elderly people, 9.6 percent of the country's total population. Combine these demographics with the World Health Organization [WHO] data that shows immunization against seasonal influenza reduces severe illness and complications by up to 60 percent and deaths by 80 percent among the elderly and you will start to see influenza as an all-too-common preventable cause of illness, hospitalization and death among the elderly.

Poor Vaccination Record

With these striking facts in mind, deciding how to ensure the elderly live healthy and active lives is not only the right thing to do, it also makes sense in terms of managing a country's health care resources.

Sadly, in many countries across Asia, these facts are either not known or overlooked. Therefore very few elderly people get vaccinated each year against seasonal influenza, resulting in unnecessary illness and economic costs. Today, Indonesia's elderly influenza immunization rates are particularly low with less than 1 percent of 18 million Indonesians 60 years or older receiving immunizations.

Similarly low levels of immunization are recorded in Pakistan and India, while Malaysia (at around 5 percent) and Thailand (at 15 percent) have marginally better immunization rates. Indeed, in the Asia-Pacific region, only Australia, Japan, New Zealand and South Korea have successful influenza programs covering most of their seniors.

A major challenge for seasonal influenza immunization programs is the unpredictability of influenza; some years there is a high level of influenza and other years it is lower. Yet on average each year, about 5 to 10 percent of adults and up to 30 percent of children worldwide will suffer from seasonal influenza infections, resulting in medical visits, hospitalization and death, not to mention the millions of lost work and school days. Also, studies have shown that our seniors have the highest risk of serious illness and death.

Sadly, in many countries across Asia. . . . very few elderly people get vaccinated each year against seasonal influenza, resulting in unnecessary illness and economic loss.

So how do you make the case for immunization of the elderly to politicians and health policy decision makers? One potentially powerful argument is that raising awareness and having robust annual influenza vaccination programs are important in establishing pandemic vaccination capabilities, while also helping to protect against annual epidemics.

Moving Forward

This is what more than 200 leading experts, including Indonesian representatives, discussed in Bangkok at the first Asia-Pacific Influenza Summit earlier this month [June 2012]. There was a clear consensus that Asia-Pacific vaccination levels are too low and that immediate action is needed if we are to reach WHO recommendations aiming for 75 percent vaccination of vulnerable groups by 2014. With this in mind, we agreed that the first step was to get down to business and make things happen. We need to work together on national policies for influenza vaccination and to make sure doctors, nurses and other health care workers recommend immunization to their patients and, equally importantly, get vaccinated themselves.

To assist this process, governments need to commit to providing free or subsidized vaccines to the priority groups. The last building block is for governments, experts and other stakeholders to work together to find more effective ways of communicating the impact of influenza and the benefits of vaccination to wider groups to encourage people to ask about vaccination.

The Bangkok summit was a good first step in stimulating development of policies to improve influenza vaccine uptake in high-risk groups. Now we need to move from discussion to action so as to ensure that Asia's elderly people are protected against influenza and can live long, healthy and fulfilling lives.

We need to work together on national policies for influenza vaccination and to make sure doctors, nurses and other health care workers recommend immunization to their patients.

As experts, we need to have the courage to express our views and explain them effectively. But we also need a clear commitment from officials. With the United Nations predicting that the percentage of Indonesians over the age of 60 may reach 25 percent of the population in 2050—or nearly 74 million elderly people—this is a challenge that is not going to go away.

Haiti: Don't Forget the Elderly

Integrated Regional Information Networks

Integrated Regional Information Networks (IRIN) is a humanitarian news and analysis service of the United Nations. In the following viewpoint, IRIN reports on the condition of the elderly in Haiti following the January 2010 earthquake in that country. Many of the elderly face difficulties because of stress, inability to get needed medications, or disruption of the social networks that had cared for them. IRIN says that aid organizations are working to provide resources and help for the elderly as well as for other disabled people. In conclusion, IRIN notes that in many cases the elderly can serve as a resource in times of disaster because of their experience and knowledge.

As you read, consider the following questions:

1. According to IRIN, why were nursing homes having trouble caring for all the elderly after the earthquake?
2. Why does HelpAge's Powell refer to diabetes and hypertension as a double whammy?
3. What do elderly people who are not in dire need after the quake require, according to IRIN?

Elderly people need more attention in the response to January's earthquake in Haiti and more appreciation of the role they can play in the relief effort, say aid workers.

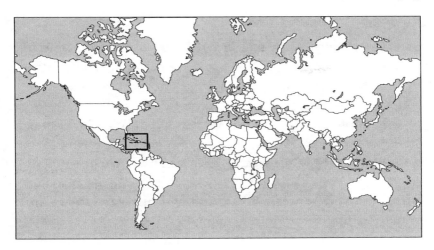

Some 800,000 Haitians, or about 7 percent of the population, are over 60, says HelpAge International and more than 200,000 elderly have been affected by the earthquake.

"It's a population that has its own specific needs and can be very vulnerable—in some ways just as vulnerable as the under-five or infant population," Cynthia Powell of HelpAge International told IRIN in the capital Port-au-Prince.

"At the same time they are adults who have had tremendously rich lives and have a lot of experience, a lot of potential to give back to society in some way."

A number of private and public nursing homes exist in the capital, HelpAge says. But they are either damaged or do not have the capacity to absorb older people discharged from hospitals or needing special care after the earthquake.

More than 200,000 elderly have been affected by the earthquake.

As part of its efforts HelpAge is working with the NGO Samaritan's Purse on a food-for-training project in which women would be trained in elderly care.

Depressed, Disoriented

In camps for displaced families IRIN saw elderly people in various conditions—from a 90-year-old woman selling laundry detergent and hand soap to a 66-year-old man who since the quake has been disoriented and refuses to eat.

"I cannot get him to eat," his daughter Yolande Casimir told IRIN, as he lay on the floor of their tent, appearing to go in and out of sleep. "He wets and soils himself. He's depressed. He talks to himself. When he gets up to walk he just falls down." She said he was diabetic and had high blood pressure, but he was fine before the earthquake.

"He is just so stressed. All he's thinking about is the house and everything else that he lost. Could you tell me what I could do to help him a little bit so he won't lose his head completely?"

Several elderly people IRIN spoke to in camps for displaced families said they had suffered chest pains and head- and stomach-aches since the quake. Most said they had high blood pressure and were no longer taking their required medicines.

"He is just so stressed. All he's thinking about is the house and everything else that he lost."

"With diabetes and hypertension it's a double whammy," HelpAge's Powell told IRIN. "After the quake there may have been an interruption in access to prescription medicines for chronic conditions like that, and both of those conditions are exacerbated by stress."

Rita Baptiste, 65, said she had an eye operation just before the earthquake and now her eyes were irritated and she could not see well. The hospital where she would have had a follow-up was destroyed, as were her glasses.

For some elderly people in the camps—many of whom are alone, their children in the provinces or abroad—getting much-needed assistance is a challenge. Philomène Casimir, 70, told IRIN that one morning she received a card for a food distribution, but when she went to collect the food in the afternoon she was jostled by the crowds and left empty-handed. She said she dared not try again.

Special Needs

HelpAge and other NGOs plan to set up dedicated zones in new IDP camps to be formed in the coming months to address such issues.

"We are advocating for a special needs area in those camps—not just for elderly but for amputees, people who are discharged from hospitals and handicapped," Michael Andreini of HelpAge told IRIN. "So that health facilities are more accessible and so that [these groups'] security and protection is taken into consideration."

A member of the committee running one camp, who gave his name only as Harold, said the breakdown of communities since the disaster meant people who might previously have paid a visit to an elderly person to lend a hand in the house or give a bit of food or money, no longer did so.

Not all elderly people affected by the earthquake were in dire need, aid workers and camp residents pointed out. Many are active and simply need to be supported with health care, food and shelter so as not to slide into vulnerability. They are also great resources, Andreini said.

"These are people who have gone through a number of different regimes, who have [been part of] the history of Haiti, who understand what it has gone through and what its potential is," he said. "Some of the best people to help plan how to rebuild this country are people who have been here for a long time."

Periodical and Internet Sources Bibliography

The following articles have been selected to supplement the diverse views presented in this chapter.

Eran Bendavid, Nathan Ford, and Edward J. Mills	"HIV and Africa's Elderly: The Problems and Possibilities," *AIDS*, vol. 26, July 31, 2012.
Denis Campbell	"Elderly NHS Patients' Harrowing Plight Is Revealed in Report," *Guardian*, February 14, 2011.
E! Science News	"Obesity Rise Linked to Disability Increase Among Elderly in Latin America and the Caribbean," July 27, 2010. http://esciencenews.com/articles/2010/07/27/obesity.rise.linked.disability.increase.among.elderly.latin.america.and.caribbean.
Karen Howlett	"Integrating Health Care Necessary for an Aging Population," *Globe and Mail*, July 10, 2011.
John Rudolf	"Elderly Inmate Population Soared 1,300 Percent Since 1980s: Report," *Huffington Post*, June 13, 2012.
Dessy Sagita	"Dearth of Immunization Among Indonesia's Elderly," *Jakarta Globe*, April 28, 2012.
Paula Span	"For Elderly Diabetics, Questions About Aggressive Care," *The New Old Age* (blog), *New York Times*, April 11, 2011. http://newoldage.blogs.nytimes.com/2011/04/11/for-elderly-diabetics-questions-about-aggressive-care.
University of Sydney	"Call for AIDS Researchers to Refocus on Elderly Africans," July 23, 2012. http://sydney.edu.au/news/84.html?newsstoryid=9672.
Timothy Williams	"Number of Older Inmates Grows, Stressing Prisons," *New York Times*, January 26, 2012.

For Further Discussion

Chapter 1

1. Julika Erfurt, Athena Peppes, and Mark Purdy identify a number of myths about population aging that they say are common. Do any of the other viewpoints in this chapter buy into or repeat these myths? Based on the viewpoints in the chapter, do any of these "myths" seem to be facts or truths rather than myths? Explain your reasoning.

2. Adam P. Smith argues that the effects of an aging population on Britain are uncertain; Ronny Linder-Ganz argues that the effects of an aging population on Israel will be disastrous. Who do you think makes a better case? Are the differences in predicted outcome due to differences in policy between Britain and Israel? Or are they due to differences in emphasis by the authors? Explain your answers.

Chapter 2

1. The viewpoints in this chapter suggest a number of policy solutions to an aging population. Which solution seems most promising? Which seems least promising? Explain your reasoning.

2. In his viewpoint, Joan Muysken suggests that encouraging immigration could help with some of the problems caused by aging. Could any of Muysken's suggested policy changes help Germany based on the viewpoint by *Spiegel?* Why or why not? Explain.

Chapter 3

1. Based on the viewpoints by Maryam Ala Amjadi and Judy Steed, are you more convinced that the elderly enjoy quality care in Denmark or in Iran? Explain your reasoning.

Chapter 4

1. Jeremy Laurance and James Ridgeway both talk about institutional government care for the elderly. What similar problems do the elderly face in the National Health Service (NHS) and the US prison system? How are solutions to these problems similar or different? Explain.

2. Based on the viewpoints by Ruthann Richter, Lance Jennings, and IRIN, influenza and earthquakes do not tend to create the same problems with orphaned elderly that the AIDS epidemic has. Why not? Are there ways in which influenza, earthquakes, and AIDS all present similar problems for elder care? Explain your reasoning.

Organizations to Contact

The editors have compiled the following list of organizations concerned with the issues debated in this book. The descriptions are derived from materials provided by the organizations. All have publications or information available for interested readers. The list was compiled on the date of publication of the present volume; the information provided here may change. Be aware that many organizations take several weeks or longer to respond to inquiries, so allow as much time as possible.

AARP
601 E Street NW, Washington, DC   20049
(888) 687-2277
website: www.aarp.org

AARP, formerly known as the American Association of Retired Persons, is a nonpartisan association that seeks to improve the aging experience for all Americans. It is the nation's largest organization of midlife and older persons, with more than thirty million members. AARP publishes the magazine *Modern Maturity* and the newsletter *AARP Bulletin*. Issue statements and congressional testimony can be found at its website.

Alzheimer's Association
225 N. Michigan Avenue, Fl. 17, Chicago, IL   60601-7633
(312) 335-8700 • fax: (866) 699-1246
website: www.alz.org

The Alzheimer's Association is committed to finding a cure for Alzheimer's disease and helping those affected by the disease. The association funds research into the causes and treatments of Alzheimer's disease and provides education and support for people diagnosed with the condition, their families, and caregivers. Position statements and fact sheets are available at its website.

Centre for Policy on Ageing

28 Great Tower Street, London   EC3R 5AT
+44 (0) 20 7553 6500 • fax: +44 (0) 20 7553 6501
email: cpa@cpa.org.uk
website: www.cpa.org.uk

The Centre for Policy on Ageing is an independent charity promoting the interests of older people through research, policy analysis, and the dissemination of information. It sponsors the international journal *Ageing & Society*. Its website includes numerous reports and reviews related to issues of aging, such as "The Future Ageing of the Ethnic Minority Population of England and Wales."

International Federation on Ageing (IFA)

351 Christie Street, Toronto, Ontario   M6G 3C3
   Canada
(416) 342-1655 • fax: (416) 392-4157
email: jbarratt@ifa-fiv.org
website: www.ifa-fiv.org

The International Federation on Ageing (IFA) is a private nonprofit organization that brings together more than 150 associations that represent or serve older persons in fifty-four nations. IFA is committed to ensuring the dignity and empowerment of older persons. It publishes the quarterly journal *Ageing International* and *Intercom*, a monthly newsletter for its members.

International Union for the Scientific Study of Population (IUSSP)

3-5 rue Nicolas, Paris cedex 20   75980
   France
+33 (0)1 56 06 21 73 • fax: +33 (0)1 56 06 22 04
email: iussp@iussp.org
website: www.iussp.org

The International Union for the Scientific Study of Population (IUSSP) promotes the scientific study of population, encourages exchange among researchers around the globe, and works to stimulate interest in population issues. It organizes seminars and training and produces a variety of publications. These include working papers, research papers, and bulletins, many of which are available through its website.

John A. Hartford Foundation
55 East Fifty-Ninth Street, 16th Floor
New York, NY   10022-1713
(212) 832-7788 • fax: (212) 593-4913
website: www.jhartfound.org

The John A. Hartford Foundation works to support efforts to improve the health of older Americans. It provides grants in numerous areas, including medical education, nursing education, and social work education. Its website includes numerous downloadable publications.

Middle East Academy for Medicine of Ageing (MEAMA)
Avenue des Alpes 37, PO Box 1112, Montreux   1820
    Switzerland
0041 21 963 01 11 • fax: 0041 21 963 60 13
email: charaf@vtx.ch
website: www.meama.com

The Middle East Academy for Medicine of Ageing (MEAMA) is an educational institution dedicated to stimulating the development of health care services for older people in the Middle East. It offers courses related to health and care of the elderly. It is a supporting organization of the *Middle East Journal of Age and Ageing*.

NGO Committee on Ageing
c/o Sanford, PO Box 20058, New York, NY   10017
(646) 831-1498
website: www.ngocoa-ny.org

The NGO Committee on Ageing works to raise global awareness of the opportunities and challenges of aging worldwide. The committee works to integrate aging in United Nations policies and programs and encourages member states to include aging in policy considerations. Its website includes reports and news related to aging issues.

United Nations Development Programme (UNDP)
One United Nations Plaza, New York, NY   10017
(212) 906-5000
website: www.undp.org

The United Nations Development Programme (UNDP) is the UN's global development network, an organization advocating for change and connecting countries to knowledge, experience, and resources to help people build a better life. The UNDP website includes documents such as "Beyond Scarcity: Power, Poverty, and the Global Water Crisis" and "The Millennium Development Goals Report 2013," which are available for download.

World Health Organization (WHO)—Ageing
Avenue Appia 20, Geneva 27   1211
    Switzerland
+ 41 22 791 21 11 • fax: + 41 22 791 31 11
email: info@who.int
website: http://www.who.int/topics/ageing/en/

The World Health Organization (WHO) is an agency of the United Nations formed in 1948 with the goal of creating and ensuring a world where all people can live with high levels of both mental and physical health. The organization researches aging issues and disseminates information on the topic. WHO publishes the *Bulletin of the World Health Organization*, which is available online, as well as the *Pan American Journal of Public Health*. It publishes reports on aging such as "Global Age-Friendly Cities: A Guide."

Bibliography of Books

Pat Armstrong et
al., eds.
A Place to Call Home: Long-Term Care in Canada. Black Point, Nova Scotia, Canada: Fernwood Publishing, 2009.

Allan Borowski,
Sol Encel, and
Elizabeth Ozanne,
eds.
Longevity and Social Change in Australia. Sydney, Australia: University of New South Wales Press, 2007.

Sara Carmel, ed.
Aging in Israel: Research, Policy and Practice. New Brunswick, NJ: Transaction Publishers, 2010.

Sheying Chen and
Jason L. Powell,
eds.
Aging in China: Implications to Social Policy of a Changing Economic State. New York: Springer, 2012.

Lisa Cliggett
Grains from Grass: Aging, Gender, and Famine in Rural Africa. Ithaca, NY: Cornell University Press, 2005.

Joan Costa-Font
Reforming Long-Term Care in Europe. Hoboken, NJ: Wiley-Blackwell, 2011.

Karen Eggleston
and Shripad
Tuljapurkar, eds.
Aging Asia: The Economic and Social Implications of Rapid Demographic Change in China, Japan, and South Korea. Stanford, CA: Walter H. Shorenstein Asia-Pacific Research Center, 2011.

Achim Goerres
The Political Participation of Older People in Europe: The Greying of Our Democracies. New York: Palgrave Macmillan, 2009.

Michele Gragnolati, Ole Hagen Jorgensen, Romero Rocha, and Anna Fruttero	*Growing Old in an Older Brazil: Implications of Population Aging on Growth, Poverty, Public Finance and Service Delivery.* Washington, DC: World Bank, 2011.
Susan M. Hillier and Georgia M. Barrow	*Aging, The Individual, and Society,* 9th ed. Belmont, CA: Wadsworth, 2011.
Sarah Lamb	*White Saris and Sweet Mangoes: Aging, Gender, and Body in North India.* Berkeley: University of California Press, 2000.
Walter Laqueur	*The Last Days of Europe: Epitaph for an Old Continent.* New York: Thomas Dunne Books/St. Martin's Press, 2007.
Ronald Lee and Andrew Mason, eds.	*Population Aging and the Generational Economy: A Global Perspective.* Northampton, MA: Edward Elgar Publishing, 2011.
John Macnicol	*Age Discrimination: An Historical and Contemporary Analysis.* New York: Cambridge University Press, 2006.
George Magnus	*The Age of Aging: How Demographics Are Changing the Global Economy and Our World.* Hoboken, NJ: Wiley, 2008.
Pranitha Maharaj, ed.	*Aging and Health in Africa.* New York: Springer, 2013.

Michael D. McNally	*Honoring Elders: Aging, Authority, and Ojibwe Religion.* New York: Columbia University Press, 2009.
Donald T. Rowland	*Population Aging: The Transformation of Societies.* New York: Springer, 2012.
Malcolm Sargeant	*Age Discrimination: Ageism in Employment and Service Provision.* Burlington, VT: Ashgate Publishing Company, 2011.
Jay Sokolovsky, ed.	*The Cultural Context of Aging: Worldwide Perspectives,* 3rd ed. Westport, CT: Praeger, 2009.
William B. Ward and Mustafa Z. Younis	*Steps Toward a Planning Framework for Elder Care in the Arab World.* New York: Springer, 2013.
Emily A. Wentzell	*Maturing Masculinities: Aging, Chronic Illness, and Viagra in Mexico.* Durham, NC: Duke University Press, 2013.
Jean Woo, ed.	*Aging in Hong Kong: A Comparative Perspective.* New York: Springer, 2013.

Index

Geographic headings and page numbers in **boldface** refer to viewpoints about that country or region.

Australian Human Rights Commission, 121

B

Baby boomers, 44, 82
Bade, Klaus J., 95
Bank of Israel, 29
Baptiste, Rita, 186
Barkat, defined, 100
Barnoski, Billy, 174
Beijing Normal University, 58
Berlin Institute for Population and Development, 95
Bhattacharya, Jay, 149
Birth control in Korea, 79
Birthrates, 12, 36–37, 88–90
Bolton NHS Trust, 142
Boston University, 176
Brazil, 61–66
Brazil, aging population
challenges to, 65
as emerging economy, 36–37
infrastructure problems, 61–66
INTERHEART international study, 161
Obstructive Lung Disease in, 163
overview, 62
sport and, 62–63
British Medical Journal, 148
Broderick, Elizabeth, 121, 123–124
Burden of disease (BOD), 156
Burstow, Paul, 145

C

Caley, M., 22, 23
Canada
GDP in, 111
home-care workers, 113

immobility of elderly, 137
older workers, 40
Cancer
colon cancer, 164
Latin America and the Caribbean, 164–165
lung cancer, 145
obesity and, 160
prevalence of, 165
stomach cancer, 142, 164
Cardiovascular disease (CVD), 158t, 161
Carter, Peter, 144
Casimir, Philomène, 187
Casimir, Yolande, 186
Centenarian demographics, 49
Centers for Disease Control and Prevention (CDC), 156, 158
Centre for Development Studies in Thiruvananthapuram, 136
Chiang Mai University, 13
Chile, 161, 163
China, 54–58, 126–131
aging in, 36–37
inverted family pyramids, 35
material necessities, 57–58
one-child policy, 54–58
too many elderly, 55–56
China, elderly assistance
falling down, deaths, 127–128
fear of helping, 128–130
lawsuit fears, 126–131
Ministry of Health guidelines, 130–131
old-age dependency ratio, 129
overview, 126–127
China Ageing Development Foundation, 57
China National Committee on Ageing, 58
China Philanthropy Research Institute, 58